COWBOY RESCUE

BARB HAN

TORJAKE PUBLISHING

Editing: Ali Williams

Cover Design: Jacob's Cover Designs

❀ Created with Vellum

To my family for unwavering love and support. I can't imagine doing life with anyone else. I love you guys with all my heart.

1

J ack McGannon leaned a hip against the side of his pickup truck, then crossed his legs at his ankles. He fished his cell from the front pocket of his jeans, questioning why he'd volunteered to take this assignment. Traffic had been a nightmare on the highway. Weather was moving in. Seeing the condition of the mares he was about to rescue was going to be a gut punch.

This so-called animal sanctuary became a prison after the owner retired, turning the family business over to a son who couldn't care less about the animals, the property, or the house from the looks of it. There had to be a special place in hell for folks who abused or neglected innocent animals.

The storm brewing outside had nothing on Jack's mood, which was darkening by the minute. But then he hadn't been in the right mindset since receiving an unsettling text from one of his exes yesterday.

Jack fisted his free hand, thinking he definitely should have taken a pass on this one.

Before he could thumb through his contacts for Texas

Parks and Wildlife, Warden William Sparks came around the side of the seventies ranch-style home. In his late thirties, most would describe him as tall and lanky with a runner's build. He stared at the ground, a scowl on his face.

The second he glanced up and saw Jack, he heaved a sigh and managed a smile. It was then Jack saw something move on the front porch. From this distance, he couldn't tell what it was.

"Afternoon, William," Jack said to his law enforcement division contact.

"Afternoon?" William cocked an eyebrow and glanced at his watch. He looked official in his department-issued all brown uniform. "I've barely had breakfast."

Jack chuckled and shook the man's hand. He guessed to some folks ten a.m. qualified as morning. "Activity starts on the ranch at four, so, yeah, ten feels late."

"Well, I guess there's probably a lot of truth to that but for us 'normal' folk, ten o'clock is still squarely in the morning."

"I haven't seen ten o'clock as a morning in..." He laughed. "Probably my entire life."

He was a natural fit for early mornings but there were parts of being a McGannon that weren't so natural. Like the whole being perfect part or when it made him a target for someone looking to cash in on his name.

"Good to see you again," William said, his tone serious now.

"How long has it been?" Jack didn't normally volunteer for pickups. He usually waited for the animals to arrive at the ranch and then rolled up his sleeves to help.

"My people are rounding up the mares. These are the last two of the bunch. My office appreciates your help in taking in animals, or finding homes for them." Jack made eye contact and held it. "I'll warn you. These two are emaciated. I can count their ribs and see their hip bones..." William took a few seconds before continuing. It was obvious how much he cared about animals. "They've been started on good quality hay in small quantity and have been given oral electrolytes and probiotics."

"I don't understand some people." Jack gestured toward the broken-down ranch-style home. Volunteering to be the one to pick up the pair of mares had given him an excuse to be off property and in the northern Austin area.

"That makes two of us." William shook his head. "But these horses just hit the ranching jackpot, if you don't mind my saying. They'll be treated like royalty from here on out."

Jack personally planned to see to it. The family vet had already been alerted and would be ready to go once Jack got the mares home.

"Hold tight," William said. "I'll bring the horses around."

Jack moved behind his trailer, opened it up and set up the ramp for the mares. He glanced over at the porch again. A dog? He took a couple of steps closer to get a better look. Thick fur and a hot Texas sun weren't exactly friends. This one looked like a Bernese Mountain and Rottweiler mix. The guy barely lifted his head up despite looking like he'd been fed. That part was a relief. Too many times animals came to the ranch that had been nearly starved to death like the mares.

William brought the horses around, so Jack turned around and moved to the trailer. True to William's word, the mares were pitiful looking. More of that anger surfaced. Jack worked to contain it.

After loading them, he closed the back doors and slid the lock to secure them. He needed to get them back to the ranch where Derek Jacobs would be waiting.

The Bernese mix lay dutifully on the porch.

"What's going to happen to that one?" He nodded toward the animal.

"I reckon he'll go to the shelter. It's not ideal and you know how much I hate taking them there," William said.

The dog moved and Jack saw a glint of metal. "What's that on him?"

"Chains. Sydney has my bolt cutters." William barely finished his sentence before Jack stalked to the pickup. He opened up the toolbox and grabbed his Kobalt fourteen-inch cutters.

"No. No. No. I'll take him with me. Maybe the familiarity of the horses and ranch life will give him comfort." The Bernese looked so sad. And maybe it was just that same internal brokenness that Jack could identify with that made him feel a draw to the animal. Either way, whether the Bernese wanted to spend the rest of his days resting and lounging around or working, it didn't matter a bit to Jack. He went into it for the long haul.

Before William could respond, Jack was stalking toward the chained-up animal. He muttered a few curses as he walked straight up to the animal.

"Might be tough to get him to move. I get the sense he's been living on that porch for most of his life," William stated. "And he'll most certainly have fleas. You sure you want to deal with that on your ride home?"

"He's been through enough already. I'll cope with the fleas if I can give him a better life." Fleas could be dealt with. Walking away from a dog that was chained on a porch wasn't something Jack could live with. He took a risk in getting up close and personal with a strange dog. The Bernese looked defeated. More of that anger surfaced.

"Just checking," William said. "Plus, I had a feeling you'd

say something like that. I don't think he's moved since we've been here."

"Is he old?" Jack positioned the cutters and then with a grunt, sliced through the chain.

"Doesn't seem so. As you can see, he is gentle, though. A vet could give a better idea of his age, but I wouldn't say that he's much older than four or five. It can't help being left out here in the heat. And his fur is matted."

"Nothing a little shampoo can't cure." Same as with the fleas. It'd be easy enough to wash him. Jack might not know what to do about the texts from his ex, but animals were second nature to him. He called to the dog to gauge how difficult it was going to be to get the Bernie to move.

The guy didn't even lift his head up.

"Hey, boy." Jack's chest took a hit when the saddest brown eyes stared up at him. The dog's head didn't move but his tail wagged, and that was a good sign.

Considering his ears didn't rear back and his disposition didn't change one bit, Jack had a lot of confidence in moving forward. True enough, up close his hair was matted. And, yes, there would be fleas. Jack had no doubts about it. A quick flea dip would help with those.

Jack fished his cell from his pocket. He snapped a pic of the Bernese and sent it to Derek, alerting him to a need for a once-over on the animal. Those eyes would haunt him forever, especially if he walked away.

"Hey, buddy," he started after replacing his phone. "How about you come home with me? What do you think?"

He searched for any signs of life in the dog and was heartbroken when the animal seemed ready to accept whatever happened. His spirit had to be pretty broken to allow that.

The Bernese didn't have on a collar, just a chain around

his neck. Since all the other animals had been seized from the property based on neglect, it was an easy case to justify taking him home to the ranch.

Getting him to stand up of his own free will was important to Jack. It would also rule out any physical injuries that might need to be looked at right away. Derek was on notice and would make sure all the necessary supplies were available. But the dog wasn't budging.

What Jack needed was a treat. Since he didn't carry around a treat bag in his pocket, he figured a pinch of meat from the sandwich Miss Penny had packed and insisted he bring would have to do. He could pinch off a piece or two of ham and see if he could get the dog to follow him to the truck. Normally, Jack drove a Jeep. This truck belonged to the ranch and was the best hookup for the trailer.

It had a big sticker on the back that said McGannon Herd, which he didn't use for his personal vehicle. Being a McGannon already placed a big enough target on his back. He didn't feel the need to blast his whereabouts. It was also the reason he didn't have any social media accounts. Not that he was the type to use them. Jack needed to be outside. He'd rather have reins in his hands than a device. He needed to breathe fresh air and feel the sunshine on his face. And right now, he needed to head back to the truck and grab that sandwich.

"No luck?"

Jack shook his head as he opened the passenger door.

"I have a secret weapon, though." The still fresh sandwich was right where he left it.

A few seconds later, he was within spitting distance of the Bernese...holding out a treat. Bernie seemed like a good name. Yeah, Jack liked that name. "What do you think? Bernie?"

Bernie with the big brown eyes didn't have much in the way of a response. So, Jack held out the bit he pinched off within a foot of the big guy's nose. And...nothing.

Jack flattened his right hand and held it even closer, so the dog could get a good whiff in case the wind had shifted. The move got Bernie's attention. Head to one side, he licked Jack's hand, then nibbled the bite.

"Good boy, Bernie." He needed to get used to his new name. New name for a new life.

Jack tore off another pea-sized treat. Bernie got the hang of this quickly, scooting closer to Jack's hand this time.

"Do you want more?" Jack took a step back and pinched off another piece. He held it on the palm of his hand.

Bernie moved, forcing himself to stand with what looked like great effort. Possible hip dysplasia, Jack thought. It wasn't uncommon in extra-large dogs. Leaving it untreated was akin to abuse. Jack had every bit of understanding for folks who couldn't afford veterinary care; his mother had started a charity for those situations. And there were rescue operations that would help; there was literally no reason to leave a dog to suffer with all the resources out there. And, sometimes, surrender was the kindest option. This place, though, was riddled with neglect.

White-hot anger tore through Jack at the animal's suffering. He also had a dilemma. He could open the trailer and put the ramp down, so Bernie could load up in the back. Or, he could risk picking Bernie up to place him in the passenger seat.

The trailer was a four-stall, and the horses were secured in the front two. Jack didn't like the idea of Bernie being back there even though it would help with the flea problem later. He could make a bed out of horse blankets, but Bernie could end up being jostled around. The other idea was a little riskier.

"Hold on there." William caught onto Jack's plan.

"I won't push him. If he doesn't want me picking him up, I won't do it." Jack had left the passenger door open. He glanced at William. "Do you mind grabbing a couple of blankets from the backseat and making a bed for him on the passenger side?"

"Sure thing." William did the favor.

"Thank you."

"Be careful with him. We both know a hurt animal is cap—"

"He's fine. Promise. I won't do anything stupid." He moved closer to Bernie. "Hey, buddy. All I want to do is get you safely inside the truck. What do you think about it?"

Given Bernie's sheer size, he could deliver a sharp bite. Jack had no intention of needing rabies shots. The image of a long needle in his stomach took hold, causing his body to shiver involuntarily. He had no idea if rabies shots still required those needles and had no intention of finding out today.

As long as he was careful, and Bernie wasn't giving any signs of agitation, Jack could move forward. The dog would only bite out of fear or protection. It was plain to see this guy didn't have a mean bone in his body. Jack managed to maneuver close enough to secure a hand underneath Bernie's front section. All that got was a face lick. Good response.

"Almost there," he soothed. It was the hindquarters he worried about. He used as calm and consistent voice as he could, knowing full well animals often took their cues from humans. Especially domestic animals. "You're doing great."

Scooping the dog up, Jack tensed, half-expecting the

worst. He moved quickly to the vehicle and placed Bernie on top of the folded blankets. He eased his hands out from underneath the hefty animal.

"Ever think about changing professions?" William blew out a breath like he'd been holding it the entire walk over.

"Nope."

"If you ever do, my office could use a few good people like you." William was only half-joking, based on the knowing look he gave.

"You know me. Ranching's in the blood. Animals are part of the job." While most ranchers used trucks to herd cattle and ATVs to check fences, McGannon Herd Cattle Ranch still rode horses. A few of the hands had converted to electronic or gas-powered, but Clive McGannon was a renaissance man. He'd taught his sons and nephews the old-fashioned way and they'd embraced it. There was something about starting his day in the saddle that righted the world.

"Hope this creep gets locked away for a long time." Jack nodded toward the house. There were a few choice words that came to mind, words much stronger than *creep*. Jack bit his tongue.

"We should be solid on this one."

Jack clenched his back teeth. William wasn't lying. Jack could literally count the mares' ribs as he'd loaded them. Disgusting. His faith in humanity was at an all-time low at the moment.

"You're good to come all the way out here, Jack," William said.

"Don't start that kind of rumor. You'll ruin my bad-boy reputation," Jack teased. He wasn't so sure about the *good* part. He stuck his right hand out between him and William, who took it and gave a good shake.

"It'll kill your dating life," William shot back.

Too soon, Jack thought. Besides, he'd done a great job of that on his own and the comment stung more than he wanted it to. He walked over to the driver's seat, climbed in, and was back on the road toward home where he belonged a minute later.

There weren't a lot of vehicles on this stretch of road, so seeing a hitchhiker out here caught his eye. She had on jean shorts and a tan-colored cotton shirt with her cowgirl boots. Her long legs weren't the only things that he noticed. She wore a wide-brimmed hat that looked incredibly familiar. Boots and a backpack never looked better on a person. Thick, wavy hair that fell halfway down her back blew in the breeze.

Out of nowhere, she turned and tucked her hand in her pocket.

Pulling up beside her, he asked, "Natalie?"

2

"Never mind," Natalie told Jack, mortified that she ran into him of all people. Wasn't that the perfect example of how her luck had always run? Since Murphy's Law was a heck of a lot more predictable than Texas weather, she chalked the current situation up to a cruel twist of fate.

"You had your thumb out. You must need a ride somewhere." His deep voice had the kind of low rumble that washed over her, bringing body parts to life that didn't need reviving. Not that it took a lot to be awestruck by Jack McGannon. He had the kind of rugged good looks that had women lining up for the chance to spend time with him.

"Not anymore." She didn't dare look at him. Not while he still had a face of hard angles and sharp planes or the kind of penetrating eyes that made her think he could see right through her.

She kept walking and he kept pace with his truck. Not exactly his truck. This one was the family owned and had thrown her off when she'd seen it coming. Jack drove a green Jeep. One that blended into the Texas scenery. So, the truck threw her.

"Come on." The truck slowed and she made a right turn toward the barbed wire fence. And since Murphy was having his way with her, there was no easy escape there, either.

Gravel crunched underneath tires as she heard Jack pull over and then stop. Since jumping a barbed wire fence was out of the question, she spun in the opposite direction toward the street. There was more barbed wire fence going the other way. Wasn't this turning out to be a red-letter day?

"Go away, Jack," she warned. "I don't need anything from you."

"I think we both know you made that clear when you left." The anger in his voice cut right through her. She hated hurting him. "Sorry. Don't listen to that. I'm not mad. I don't care about the past. But I am concerned that you're going to end up in trouble out here on the side of the road. Do you realize pedestrian deaths are one of the leading killers in this state? Or are you so stubborn that you're willing to—"

"To what?" She whirled around on him. Big mistake. His six-feet-five-inches of rock- toned muscle gave him an intimidating physical presence. She had to look up to look into his eyes—pale blue, hooded with the thickest black lashes she'd ever seen.

Being anywhere close in physical distance to him knocked her off-kilter. At this distance, she breathed in his spicy male scent and she could've sworn fireworks lit up the ever-darkening sky.

"End up hurt or dead to prove a point?" He crossed his arms over a broad chest. "Hitchhiking, Natalie? Seriously? You want a random guy in a truck to pick you up? Someone who could have a load of guys inside waiting to do God knows what to a beautiful woman?"

The move had been desperate. She'd give him that. No way would she have gotten inside a vehicle full of strangers, though, or anyone who looked sketchy. Best case would be a female driver. And, yes, women drove trucks. Jack knew that too. He wasn't making a sexist remark. His concern for her had been evident in his voice, whereas she'd been running on pure adrenaline since yesterday morning.

"I have a weapon, Jack." The kitchen knife in her backpack was all the protection she would need if someone didn't take the hint and move on if she asked them to.

"And what if someone stronger than you takes it away? What if said person uses it against you?" His normally full lips thinned. The day-old stubble on his chin meant he was working long hours. On closer inspection, there were dark circles cradling his eyes and his hair looked like it needed a good cut. He stabbed his fingers through it like he was trying to tame the wild strands.

"Okay. Point taken. Now, will you go?" The words came out harsher than she intended.

If he was offended, he didn't flinch. "I'm not leaving until you tell me why you're out here alone."

Because she couldn't use her credit card anywhere, not even for a car service after her car died, but she couldn't tell him. A response like that one would lead to more unwanted questions about her personal life. Case closed.

"Where's your husband?" Jack asked, and she flinched on his last word. The gold band on her left finger felt like a vise that had been tightened a few notches too tight. She flexed and released her fingers a few times to ease some of the tension.

"Fiancé," she quickly corrected. A little too quickly based on his reaction. "And we're having trouble right now."

The intensity of Jack's expression ratcheted up a few notches. "What kind of trouble?"

Before she could answer, he put a hand up to stop her. "Tell me the truth, Natalie. Is he hurting you?"

She twisted the ring around her finger a few times as she sucked in a breath. "No. Not physically. Nothing like that. We're in a fight right now. That's all. A disagreement."

It didn't help matters when Jack's gaze started perusing her face, then neck. Wherever those blue eyes moved left a hot trail on her skin. The sobering thought he was looking for bruises didn't stop her pulse from pounding at the base of her throat. Or her heart to freefall like she was base jumping.

"Has he ever threatened you in any way?" Jack's genuine concern was making this harder than she wanted it to be.

No. No. No. Her fake fiancé hadn't threatened her or laid a hand on her or made her feel the least bit uncomfortable. He hadn't done any of those things because he didn't exist. But there was someone out there who wanted her to disappear. A very dangerous person, who would slash her throat for going to the police again.

"Um, sorry, Jack. I'm not representing myself very well, am I?" She hemmed and hawed, trying to buy time to think up a good excuse. Why was it the best lines came to her long after a conversation like this was over? In the moment, it was much harder to come up with an excuse.

He didn't budge. All he did was shake his head.

"Okay, so, I appreciate your concern." Before he could cut her off, she brought a hand up to stop him. "No, really. I do. More than you realize." Seeing him was hard. Did he have to be so damn gorgeous? Honest? Caring? Perfect?

Lying to him before had kept them both safe. There was no way she could go back on her word now. Nothing had changed. Jack was the kind of guy who would want to help her. In doing so, he could end up dead and it would be her fault. Sorry. She wasn't going down that road again. Been there. Done that. Threw away the T-shirt.

"Then, tell me why you're here and what I can do to help." Did he have to be so damn decent? Call it The Cowboy Code, but Jack McGannon had more than his fair share of it.

Shoring up her resolve, she mustered as calm of an attitude as she could before saying, "There's nothing. I'm fine now. I was just being lazy because I'm wearing boots and I didn't want to keep walking."

"Did he abandon you here?" Jack looked up one side of the road before looking down the other. His voice hummed with anger.

"He's coming back," she lied. Lying was awful. It made her chest squeeze. She'd never been very good at it. But then, someone else's life had never depended on her selling a lie before. Rather than stand there and risk giving herself away, she started down the two-lane road again.

"Natalie. Would you stop walking away from me for a minute?" There was no anger in his voice now, just pleading. It was enough to make her stop.

She issued a sharp breath, planted her fist on her side, and turned to face him. Even with a good five feet between them, she could feel the draw. Their chemistry had zinged off the charts and not even time had dimmed the heat pinging between them.

Jack leaned a hip against his truck and crossed his arms over his chest. Standing there like he was caused her heart to freefall. She didn't walk away three months ago because she stopped feeling attracted to him. That was for sure. The intensity of their relationship had caught her off guard. There was something fearless and freeing about knowing what she wanted and going for it. And she'd gone for it with careless abandon. But that's when she thought she was dating Jack Gannon, a nobody who worked on a ranch.

"You lied to me, Jack." Boy, did she feel like a hypocrite for saying those words. Although, she'd never once lied to him while they were dating. Well, that wasn't exactly true. She hadn't told him her real name. But she *was* Natalie Baker now. There was no going back to her old life.

"I didn't lie about who I am," he argued.

"Your last name is a pretty big deal," she countered. "I'd say concealing that from me is lying about who you are. Wouldn't you?"

She was trying to push his buttons by arguing, frustrate him so he'd walk away. Nothing in his body language said he'd shy away from this discussion. He was more stubborn than she realized, and this was not going to be easy. Especially considering the effect he was having on her body.

A warm blush crawled up her neck, flushing her cheeks. She hoped keeping her distance would block him from noticing.

Too late, she realized. And now she really was in trouble.

"Okay, that one is on me. I'm not upfront with new people about who I am." Jack had learned the hard way that it was best to keep his true identity a mystery until he trusted someone enough to reveal his last name. Honestly, his relationships didn't usually make it that far. And it was probably just his bruised ego at being rejected that had him unable to let this one go. Truth was, he still thought about Natalie on a near-daily basis. "If it makes a difference, I was going to tell you."

"Really? When?" Seeing Natalie again reminded him just how much he missed her. He missed waking up to her long, honey-colored hair splayed across his pillow, their legs tangled in the sheets. He missed her flowery and clean scent on his blankets. And he missed the spark in those cobalt blue eyes that were like looking at a rare gem.

"Soon." It was a pretty lame response. "It takes time for me to trust someone enough to tell—"

Hells bells if that wasn't the exact wrong thing to say. Her nostrils flared and he practically saw steam shoot out of her ears.

"Are you kidding me right now?"

Trust didn't come easy for him, but he'd been willing to go there with her. He'd wanted to take the next step of getting to know each other on a deeper level.

"I should've said something sooner," he admitted, but he refused to apologize for dropping the first two letters of his last name early on in a relationship. Knowing he was a McGannon from Texas made it too difficult to stay under the radar when dating. He was already dealing with the latest paternity claim, another attempt to score some of his family's fortune.

"Water under the bridge," she said with a finality that said she didn't do second chances. It was probably his bruised ego that had him wanting to know if his last name was the real reason for the split.

"I'd like to make it right between us," he said.

A half-laugh, half-chortle came out of her mouth.

"And how do you propose to do that? You can't exactly undo a lie and I'm already seeing someone else."

"Nope. I can't. You could let me restart as a friend." True. He couldn't go back and fix what he'd done. But the last woman he dated before Natalie secretly recorded him to put on social media. Proof, he guessed, they'd gone out. The secret recordings and baby claims left a sour taste in his mouth. Trust took time.

Jack might come from a wealthy family, but he worked the ranch as hard as anyone else and took great pride in his contributions. He earned his keep, so being pinned as some kind of celebrity catch because his bank account had a bunch of zeroes in it was enough to turn his stomach.

So, yeah, he fudged his name until he got to know someone. And, no, he didn't trust a whole lot of people who didn't already share the same last name. He wouldn't apologize for refusing to make the same mistakes over and over again after being burned by past dates. He'd learned his lesson and adjusted accordingly.

Besides, people made a bigger deal out of his family's money than necessary. Not one of his brothers or cousins drove expensive cars or lived in mansions. They worked alongside the ranch's foreman and hands. Each pulling their weight and taking great pride in it.

"Will you at least let me explain why I did it?" He hoped so because he felt a deep need to help her understand.

"Free country."

"I don't care about what the country does. I care about you." His last four words got her attention. The shift might have been subtle, but he caught it. The slight tilt of her head that meant she was actually starting to listen. The way her stance relaxed ever so slightly. Small cues, but signs of progress.

"Go ahead then. I'm standing here, aren't I?" She wasn't going to make this easy on him, though.

"I got tired of people caring more about my last name than they did me." That was as succinct as he could put it.

The spark returned to her cobalt blues. "Was I that kind of person to you?"

"No. Of course not."

"I'll believe that after you sell me a bridge—"

"You don't have to believe it to make it true. But it is the truth." He knew she had no way of reading his mind and his actions clearly gave her the impression he'd lumped her in the same bucket as the others. He'd known from the beginning she was special. How special? It took time to figure out. He'd ignored his instincts—instincts that told him she could be trusted—in favor of experience.

"Convince me then." The challenge she issued was a no-win situation. The ring on her left hand meant he would keep a safe distance. His heart would take another hit being around her, but he wanted to make up for the past.

"Where are you headed?" He glanced over at the truck, hoping Bernie was doing okay.

She blinked at him like he'd just asked for her social security number. There wasn't much he could do except come clean about his situation.

"I have a very large, injured dog in my truck and two mares in the back who've been suffering from criminal neglect. I need to get all three of these guys back to the ranch as soon as possible so they can start receiving the care each deserves. So, I'm not trying to blow you off here or come off as impatient. I care about what happens to you, Natalie. It's as simple as that. I wish you could believe me."

"I do." The words came out small and he barely heard them.

"Then, can I take you somewhere? Drop you off where

it's safe? Because I can't drive away from here unsure of where that leaves you."

"You headed straight home?" One of her eyebrows came up.

He nodded.

"What about that spare bedroom in your house on the property? Is it still empty?" she continued.

"It is."

"Can I crash there for a few days?" She let her guard slip for the briefest second but he saw a vulnerability there that caused his protective instincts to flare up.

"Yes."

"Promise not to tell anyone?" Her head tilted to one side again and it was a good sign.

"I won't tell a soul," he promised. "The ranch has been turned upside down recently anyway. Everyone's distracted. You should be able to slip right in unnoticed and stay under the radar."

"What happened?" Concern wrinkled her forehead and it was the cutest damn thing he'd ever seen.

"My dad had an accident and has been in the hospital ever since." He didn't feel the need to go into more details about it at the moment.

"I'm so sorry, Jack. Will he be okay?" Her genuine concern told him the person he'd fallen for was very much alive inside the frigid outer shell.

"He's doing better now," he said. "Are you coming?"

"Honestly, I can use a few days away from here." Was she relenting? Taking him up on his offer of assistance? Good. For reasons he didn't want to try to explain, he wanted to help her.

"One thing, though." She locked gazes with him and he took a shot to the heart, a reminder of how painful losing her had been. Only three months had passed, and he still felt the pinch.

"Name it." *Within reason.*

"No pictures of me or mentions on social media."

"Nothing's changed, Natalie. I still don't have any of those accounts." Jack laughed. As far as odd requests went, that qualified as a doozy. It also piqued his interest about her fiancé and brought up even more questions about her situation.

3

"Is this the injured animal you mentioned earlier?" Natalie opened the door to the passenger seat and a massive dog blinked up at her. She'd have to cup two hands together to hold his chin based on the size of his head.

"Careful with him. He's a sweetheart but you never know what might happen with an animal in pain. He might snap at you without meaning to hurt you." Jack slid the blankets to the middle of the vehicle, gently taking the hundred plus pound dog with them. "Fair warning, he probably has fleas."

"Poor baby." Head down, grimace on his face, he looked to be in pain. She climbed in next to him and buckled in. "Okay to touch him?"

"He's a sweetheart. Bad hips, so be careful there." Jack slid in behind the wheel. Being in the vehicle with him felt a little too right, so she reminded herself not to get too comfortable.

"Did someone hurt him?" The thought anyone could injure such a gentle giant like this one caused white-hot anger to rip through her.

"Neglect is more like it." He gripped the steering wheel a little tighter as he navigated onto the road. "I'm guessing the hips are dysplasia."

"Sounds painful. Was he born with it?" She stopped herself from reaching over to pet him, remembering about the fleas. Then again, a couple of fleas never hurt anyone if they were taken care of quickly, and this guy deserved to have physical contact. She reached over and scratched him behind the ears. He barely budged. Natalie had no idea if dogs could feel depression but that's what it looked like with this guy. He could also have a host of other health problems. Her heart literally hurt for him.

"It's genetic but can be sped up with this kind of gross neglect." His jaw muscle clenched. It was his tell when he was angry and wanted to say a whole lot more than he was. In the few months they'd dated, she'd never seen him be anything but kind to creatures big and small. In fact, he used to put out a bowl of water every morning for a feral kitten when he stayed over at her house.

When Jack had told her that he worked on a ranch, she'd taken him at face value, envisioning him sleeping in a bunkhouse with half a dozen other guys. He'd mentioned coming from a big family and, to her, big family equaled poor. She'd bonded with him over the fact she'd been poor, and he'd say things like, *there's shame in being lazy, but not in being broke.*

Looking back, he never said that *he* didn't have money. She'd made assumptions. Assumptions that he must have realized she'd made, but never corrected. And that was flat-out betrayal in her book. People had proven to be untrustworthy in her life. Finding someone honest who had her back trumped most everything else.

She understood that he was protecting himself and his

family by hiding his last name. Odd really, because she never would have dated him if she'd known who he was. He really didn't have to worry about her coming after him for his bank account.

The timing of the breakup was awful because she'd fallen for him. Hard. If only she'd figured it out sooner before her heart had gone all-in. That was unfortunate on her part.

She glanced down and realized she'd been twisting the band on her ring finger. She flattened her palm against the seat and tucked her hand underneath her leg, so betrayal wouldn't stare back up at her. Since she wasn't ready to talk about it and she really did want to know about his dad, she shifted gears. "You mentioned that your dad was injured. What happened?"

"He took a spill inside the equipment room and smacked his head on the concrete hard enough to put him in a coma."

She covered her gasp with her right hand. "That's terrible. I'm so sorry, Jack."

"Thankfully, he's awake now. It's a new development but all signs are encouraging that he'll recover all motor function."

"That must've been a scary time." Although, she figured Jack would never admit to being scared of anything. And he probably wasn't considering his size and general physical condition. The man made an ox look weak. He had that rare combination of drop-dead gorgeous looks, intelligence, and a body made for sinning. On top of all that, he had a sense of humor. Or maybe he just understood hers, not that anything had been funny for a long time since their breakup.

Jack had been a preverbal oasis in the desert. The right

person with the right conditions matching up. Natalie wasn't sure if she could do forever with anyone, but she could see herself spending a long time ridiculously happy with Jack. Or should she say *broke* Jack? Rich and well-known Jack was far too much of a risk.

"I'm just grateful he's doing better. He's too young and strong to..." His voice trailed off and she realized emotion was getting to him. Instinct or maybe it was habit had her reaching for his arm to comfort him. The dog in between them didn't move a muscle but physical contact with Jack sent a current rippling through her hand and up her arm.

It had caught her off guard the first time they met. After a month of dating, she'd come to expect it. Getting used to it would be asking too much. She shoved those thoughts aside temporarily. Their chemistry had always been off the charts. Good to know nothing had changed, she thought wryly.

"It sounds like a miracle that he's going to fully recover." She refocused.

"It is. Doc said he'd seen this happen before with head trauma patients, but not often enough for it to be considered normal. It's a blessing for sure." She noted that his arm had tensed with contact a few seconds ago and she couldn't help but wonder if he felt the electricity as strongly as she did. Their attraction had been explosive from the get-go. Instead of a blaze that burned out just as fast, it had morphed into a slow burn. One that simmered constantly and apparently needed very little stoking to get going again.

And since thinking about it was making her cheeks flame again, she redirected her thoughts for what felt like the fifth time. "I'm sure you and your bro..." Hold on a second. She didn't actually know if his siblings were all boys like he'd said.

"Brothers and cousins. All boys," he said. "The only thing I fudged was my last name."

"And the fact that you're filthy rich." She hadn't meant to say those words out loud.

"My family is. And, yes, I have more zeroes in my bank account than a person needs, but I earn my own way and spend what I make." The mix of pride and defensiveness in his voice said she'd stepped on a landmine.

"You don't have to explain yourself to me. I never thought you were a trust-fund kid. And, honestly, I never cared." It was the fact that he came from such a high-profile family that she couldn't live with. Money was nice and, believe her, she wished she had more of it. The green stuff came in handy. Or, should she say plastic? Seemed like everyone used credit cards nowadays.

"Good. But that doesn't exactly explain why you left me when you found out that I was one." More of that hurt laced his tone and it pierced her protective wall.

"I don't want to talk about it." Now. Or ever. The less he knew, the better off he'd be. Dating a high-profile guy like Jack would thrust her into the limelight, like it or not. Out *there*, Thibaut Fontenot would find her. Well, not him exactly, because he'd been locked behind bars for his crimes thanks, in part, to her testimony. She'd been protected as a witness until the trial. Not long after, she'd been cut loose from the program. Once Fontenot had been murdered in prison, she didn't need to be protected from him.

The problem was that Fontenot had a son, Roch, who'd lost a father and a sizable income after his dad's incarceration then death at the hands of a rival. So, the Fontenot family blamed her for their financial losses. Total no-win situation. Because once she was cut loose from the program, she was on her own. She got to keep her new identity, Natalie Baker, and the job she loved at a children's hands-on museum in Austin. She worked on the nightshift, cleaning and sanitizing all the objects. She made sure every piece of equipment was in good working order for the following day's guests. And, most importantly, she got to work behind the scenes and while the world slept.

Then there were Tuesdays, her nights off, and open mic nights at a hole-in-the-wall bar on 6th Street. She loved singing and fully believed that part of her life would be over after entering the program. Basically, staying under the radar became her full-time job.

Austin was quite a few miles from the small parish in Louisiana where she'd grown up. But she'd been born in Texas and was a Texan through and through. She had always wanted to come back. Austin was her favorite city, the perfect mix of weird and busy. The influx of college students made it easy to stay unseen, especially the times she threw on a hoodie. Those helped her blend right in. Most people were shocked when they learned her true age anyway, figuring she was an undergrad student.

"My turn to ask a question." Jack's tone caused her to sit up a little straighter.

OUT OF THE corner of Jack's eye, he saw Natalie tense up. He wasn't trying to stress her out, but he had questions that needed answering.

"Not a good idea, Jack."

"I gotta ask anyway. Are you in some kind of legal trouble?"

"As in trouble with the law?" She shook her head,

sounding a little more than disappointed at the question. "I thought you knew me better than that."

"I did too but then you up and took off with almost no explanation." There had to be a reason she was hiding. If the scared look in her eyes had to do with the ring on her finger, he could help her find assistance for that. There were women's shelters that were excellent at helping women in abusive relationships. Strange, because he didn't see her as the type who would put up with abuse. But then abusers could be master manipulators. Abuse wasn't always physical, either. He'd heard emotional abuse could be just as damaging and didn't heal as quickly as a bruise might.

"There was a reason," she countered after a thoughtful pause.

"Okay." There was more to the story and she didn't look like she was going to talk about it anytime soon. Or maybe his bruised ego needed there to be more to it. He didn't want to accept that she could walk away so easily when the breakup had been so tough on him.

"No," she finally said. "I'm not in trouble with the law."

"Is your fiancé going to come looking for you?"

She hesitated before saying, "Yes. But I never mentioned you, so he won't come to..." She paused for a beat. "Where are we going anyway?"

The entire time they dated, he made the trip to Austin to see her. This was the first time she was going to see where he lived. "Specifically?"

"You know what I mean."

He wished he did. She'd been tap dancing around the real reason she'd been out on the road hitchhiking. In the past, he'd been able to read her mood with one look. Not anymore.

His cell buzzed in his pocket. Once this paternity issue

was set right, he needed to change his number again. Although he would bet money that he wasn't the father, he was concerned about the woman lobbying the accusation. Something was off, and he wanted to check into it.

"You don't want to answer that?"

"It can wait." There was no way he was having a conversation in front of her about an accusation he'd fathered a child. Susan's calls were coming in a little too regularly and she was sounding a little more desperate each time. Normally, he could wait out an accusation like this one. Time being the great equalizer. Wait long enough and like a car that ran out of gas, momentum would slow and eventually stop. All he ever requested—all he ever had to request —was proof in the form of a paternity test, which usually ended the discussion. Don't get him wrong, if he had a kid out there, he would step up and do the right thing. No question. That had never been the case. Being betrayed by someone he was just getting to know had gotten old fast. So, yeah, he'd built in what he considered an extra layer of protection, a bogus last name. Made it easier to sift out the celebrity seekers.

"Okay." It wasn't what she said so much as how she said it. 'Okay' was a lot like saying, 'fine.'

Not good.

She bit back a yawn and pinched the bridge of her nose.

"Seat lays back if you're tired," he said.

Without responding, she reached for the lever and leaned back. She went far enough that anyone driving by wouldn't be able to see her face. "Mind if I close my eyes for the rest of the way?"

"Not at all." His thoughts were already shooting off in several directions. First things first, he wanted to help secure Natalie out of sight. Easily accomplished on the ranch at his place. All he had to do was cancel cleaners who stopped by every other week and tell Miss Penny that he could swing by the house for food rather than have it delivered to his place.

Miss Penny kept McGannon Herd running and was more like family than employee. She'd raised Jack and the other boys, stepping in as a mother figure when theirs had died in an accident. And Miss Penny was still there, taking care of anyone who needed it along with running the big house. She'd been standing by his father's side during the entire coma ordeal. Her and the foreman, Hawk, named for the fact nothing ever got past him, had become especially close after working together the better part of thirty years. Their bond seemed even tighter lately.

Secondly, Jack wanted to neutralize any threat to Natalie. There was a possibility she'd been involved with someone long before the two of them had met. That would explain the quick engagement after she broke up with Jack. Again, it might be his ego talking but he didn't want to think she could fall for someone else so easily.

Saying those words in his head still caused him to tense up like he was getting ready to take a punch.

For the rest of the drive, he thought about how keeping her under the radar might prove more difficult than he originally believed. The situation was a little complicated considering he needed to deliver the horses and get medical care for Bernie.

Jack slowly released the breath he'd been holding as he turned onto ranch property. He also heard the steady, even breathing coming from both Natalie and his new pet. He hated to interrupt such deep sleep, but he needed her awake, so she wasn't surprised if she woke while he was in the barn.

He reached over to gently touch her on the shoulder.

She recoiled and fought back the second he made contact. Her breath came out in gasps.

"It's okay," he soothed. "It's Jack. Remember? You're safe."

Well, hells bells. He really wasn't letting her out of his sight until he knew exactly what was going on in her life that made her react like she'd just been assaulted. All he'd done was lightly touch her.

Even Bernie stirred, looking up at her with those big brown eyes.

"Sorry." She glanced around, hands touching her chest and stomach like she was checking to make sure she hadn't been shot or stabbed. That was quite a reaction for someone who'd said all she needed was a couple days break so she could go home and deal with a fight between her and a fiancé. "I'm sorry."

"Don't be."

"I just..." The panic in her eyes matched the sound of her voice.

"I needed to wake you up because we're here and there'll be a couple of ranch hands helping me unload the horses as soon as we get to the barn. If you want to stay under the radar, you're going to need to climb in the back seat and put a blanket over you. Otherwise, I'll just tell them like it is. You're a friend of mine who came to hang out for a few days. They'll assume we're together and that means they'll respect our privacy. Tell me what you want to do."

Natalie slid the ring off *that* finger and tucked it inside her backpack. She reached over and absently stroked Bernie's ears. "Will he go in the barn too?"

"I'd like to take him home with me, but my guess is that he's going to need to be evaluated in Derek's office."

Her eyebrows knitted together.

"He's the family vet."

She rubbed her eyes, like she was afraid she was dreaming. "Is this the house where you grew up?"

"Yes."

"Holy cow, Jack."

"We have a lot of those."

"A lot of what?"

"Cows."

She laughed and the sound was musical. She'd always had that melodic quality that was balm to a damaged heart.

"Thanks for laughing," he said.

"Thanks for being corny."

"Hey, it worked." He was rewarded with a smile that melted a few layers of ice around his heart. Had he become a little calloused to the world, expecting everyone to want something from him as soon as they found out he was a McGannon? The cold hard truth wasn't the one he wanted to acknowledge. Because the answer was a hard yes for him.

"Yep." She slinked back against the seat. "I knew your family was well off...but, seriously...this? The place is beyond, Jack."

"There are more important things in life than growing up in a big house."

"Yeah? Name one."

He refused to go the gooey route and say, *love,* so he went with, "Fishing."

She laughed again as he pulled up beside the barn doors.

"How 'seen' do you want to be?" he asked, wanting her to stay relaxed and comfortable around him.

"Not a whole lot."

"Done." He parked, fished his cell out of his pocket, and then fired off a text.

"What's that for?"

"I'm canceling my help. It's no problem for me to unload the mares on my own. And we can take Bernie here to my house since Derek is waiting in the barn to check out the mares first. He'll get them squared away and then he can swing by for Bernie. When he stops by, you can hide in the master bedroom."

"Guest room," she corrected. "I'm not kicking you out of your own room."

"Don't take this the wrong way, but I wasn't planning on letting you."

4

Natalie watched through the side-view mirror as Jack unloaded the mares. Her chest squeezed and her hands fisted when she saw the condition the horses were in. Tears sprang to her eyes as she struggled against the onslaught of emotion threatening to suck her underwater and spin her around. This seemed like a good time to remind herself these sweet animals would suffer no more. It ended today. Never again would they go without food or basic care. Their lives were changing for the better and they would be treated like royalty from here on out. There was comfort in the thought.

Beyond that, she was trying to wrap her mind around the size of his family's ranch. Looking around in awe, she reasoned there would be people out there who would try to take advantage of him after getting a look at this place. It explained why he didn't bring people here until he really knew them and why he hid his last name, but it didn't lessen the pain from him not trusting her.

A few years ago, she would have been even more skeptical. Now, after being forced to live with a new identity, she was beginning to understand that sometimes tough choices had to be made. To be fair, her name change was forced while he'd misrepresented his. After four months of dating, he'd kept the secret.

Looking back, a red flag should have been raised when she noticed he always used cash. Much to her embarrassment now, she assumed he had bad credit. Could she have been more wrong?

Not really.

Then there was the time she'd overheard a couple in the booth next to them out to dinner one night. Jack had excused himself to get his phone from his Jeep. At first, she thought the couple mistook him for someone else. And then she heard more whispers in the bathroom about *the* Jack being there. She let her doubts simmer until they boiled over. Back at her apartment, she confronted him. He owned up to it, but how long would their relationship have gone on with her in the dark? Weeks? Months? A year? More than that?

How long would it have taken for someone to take a picture of the two of them and put it up on social media? That's all she needed in her life. Fontenot might be dead, but his son wasn't—a son who had sworn to get revenge.

Someone, and she had one name on that list, or an underling had found her and slipped something in her coffee at Austin Grinds where she'd been studying yesterday morning. Poison? If a fly hadn't landed in her cup after she'd gotten back from the bathroom, she would be dead by now.

Her body shivered at the memory.

Once again, she needed to ditch everything familiar and prepare to start her life over. This time, she was doing it on her own terms. She couldn't risk having a file somewhere with her information inside. Not after her handler retired.

Living off the grid couldn't be too bad, could it? She wouldn't be able to use her credit cards, which would be a pain. She'd gotten so used to the convenience of them. They'd be too easy to use to track her down. No. If the Fontenot son or one of his associates figured out her new name—and, face it, how hard would it be now that they'd tracked her to Austin—her life was over. Everything was happing so fast.

A couple of days. That's all she needed to figure out her next steps. She'd been running blind for the past twenty-four hours after emptying out her bank account. From here on out, she was a cash girl. Not unlike Jack when she'd first met him.

Deciding where to go would be a good place to start. The Dakotas sounded good. Lots of land. Very few people. The winters would be brutal, and she was so not a cold weather person. There was always also New Mexico or Arizona. Too predictable?

It was probably time to shake things up and head to the northeast. Could she survive winter in a place like Delaware or New Hampshire? Her brain cramped thinking about all the changes coming her way and she was working up to a killer headache. Sleep sounded too good to be true. She'd squeezed in a cat nap on the drive, which usually did the trick. Not today. She had that still-asleep feeling, like she was in a fog and couldn't shake it.

She'd think better after a shower, a good night of sleep and a fresh cup of coffee. In that order. And food. Her stomach picked that moment to growl, reminding her that she'd been walking for hours straight before being picked up by Jack. And since she was going all in with her complaints, her feet hurt. Boots hadn't been her best choice yesterday morning and she'd been too panicked running home to scrub the place of anything that could identify her to change into more comfortable shoes. She'd trashed all her mail and emptied her file drawer in such a rush she still wasn't absolutely certain she destroyed everything.

Déjà vu struck and she remembered contemplating a big move three years ago. The same unsettled feeling in the pit of her stomach took hold. Life was about to change again. No. Life was *about* change, she reminded herself. Standing still was just an illusion. Nothing ever stayed the same.

The reminders did little to ease her anxiety of the unknown. Having a plan would help. Tomorrow. She'd come up with a plan after coffee. Life would feel better again if her future wasn't so uncertain.

Austin had been a little too good, a little too right. The city was just her pace and the tacos...don't even get her started. The tacos were perfection. Would North or South Dakota have decent tacos? How about New Hampshire?

It was probably strange to be worried about something that could seem trivial for an outsider looking in. But all those little things made up a life. Favorite coffee shop. Favorite spot to hear live music. Favorite person to wake up to...

That had been Jack and she'd had the most miserable time trying to shake him from her thoughts. How was that for irony? She hadn't even known his real name.

She was in a mood. Her thoughts were bouncing around. Today was for mourning everything she was about to lose. Tomorrow was for fresh starts.

"Right, boy?" She looked to the sleepy animal. The dog craned his neck around, and she could've sworn he winced with movement. Her heart went out to him. He seemed docile and like a gentle giant. He deserved to be cared for and loved. "You just found yourself the best possible home, buddy."

The sentiment caused tears to blur her vision. She sniffed them back, thinking the dog wasn't the only one who needed either of those things.

"What do you think, boy?" She needed to ask Jack for his dog's name.

Speaking of Jack, he unhitched the trailer and then reclaimed the driver's seat a few minutes later.

She sniffed back waterworks trying to push past her resolve. This wasn't the time or place to lose it, no matter how quickly emotion was building like a tsunami.

"That didn't take long," she said to Jack, thinking again that she never would have known by his laid-back disposition that he came from money. He had the rough hands of a laborer. They were one of many reasons he could sell the lie so easily. The thought of how incredible those hands had felt on her body wasn't doing her any favors. It also caused her to blush and heat to circle low in her belly. She blamed her reaction on exhaustion and hunger.

"Not my first rodeo," he quipped and then fired off a wink that could melt the toughest resolve. Why did he have to be so good at making her smile? And why did he have to be so damn charming?

"I saw you talking to a guy through the rearview mirror. Is he the vet?"

Jack nodded. "He'll be over to check out Bernie as soon as he does a workup on the mares."

"I don't want to trouble you, but…"

"You couldn't. What do you need?" His quick response convinced her that he was sincere.

"It's just you're a single guy and bachelors with food in

the fridge are basically unicorns, so—" She stopped when his laugh cut her off.

"I have food," he stated. "In defense of bachelors everywhere, I also have help with my meals. You never met Miss Penny because we didn't get the chance to come here, but she's the reason this place runs as smoothly as it does. She cooks and brings food around to all of our houses and makes sure we don't die of hunger."

"So, the part about you having all those brothers and cousins. You said it before, but I'm just fact-checking. Is it true?"

He issued a sharp sigh.

"Yes." One-word answers were never a good sign. She'd learned the hard way in past relationships.

Her stomach growled again. Louder this time. Embarrassingly enough, it managed to stop all conversation.

"Between the two of us, I highly doubt I'm the one with all the secrets." Didn't those words strike a chord? Guilt stabbed her in the center of the chest because he was right. She had secrets—secrets that could kill him if Fontenot's son found out Jack was hiding her. There was no amount of money that could stop the criminal mind on a mission. Jack was taking a risk that he didn't even realize he was taking. Her fault, and she needed to make it right. But how?

Tell him the truth and she highly doubted he was the type who could give her a meal, a roof over her head for a night, and then let her walk away. He would feel compelled to help. She didn't need to know his last name to realize that. She knew *him*.

Don't tell him and he could end up in the crosshairs. Could she find a way to tell him without revealing the whole story?

She had to find a way. The danger was real. He needed to know.

"I have to tell you something and I don't want you to freak out."

~

"CAN IT WAIT?" Jack pulled up to his log-cabin style two-story home. As interesting as Natalie's statement sounded, he had something else on his mind. Bernie. Getting him out of the truck without triggering the pain in his hips would require a lot of careful maneuvering.

"Sure." Did she just sigh relief?

Jack made a mental note to circle back to her news once Bernie was settled.

"I need to get him to the enclosed back porch with as little pain as possible." He cut the engine off and then set the keys onto the floorboard.

"What do you need me to do?" She stared at the spot where he'd placed the keys.

"Open and close a few doors." Jack exited the vehicle and then slid the blanket toward the driver's door, figuring that was all the help he needed from her. "You're gonna be just fine, Bernie."

She smiled and his heart took a hit. Jack had to admit having her at the ranch felt a little too right, especially considering the gold band tucked inside her backpack. She'd said fiancé, not husband. Trying to rationalize which was better was a losing game. Either way, she was committed to someone else.

"He is now," Natalie said. Her confidence in him didn't help matters.

Bernie didn't have a collar on, so Jack figured any name

was fair game. Plus, Bernie was getting a fresh start and Jack didn't want to be associated with anything the dog had been called in the past. His new life started now.

"I like his name, by the way." She smiled, warming dangerous places inside Jack. Places best left dormant. And he shouldn't let himself feel a sense of satisfaction that Natalie liked the name he picked out for his new pet. He also shouldn't get too used to having her around. This was a short-term arrangement. *Temporary*, he reminded. She was only there long enough to get her bearings. The thought crossed his mind that he needed to talk her out of the engagement. Any guy she felt like she had to run away from couldn't be the right one for her.

"He's a good boy. Aren't you, Bernie?" Fenagling the dog out of the front seat without tweaking his hips was going to take some finesse. So, Jack refocused.

Natalie came around the front of the truck and stood by his side. Her elbow grazed his arm and frissons of heat traveled through him. *Way to keep feelings on the down low, McGannon.*

Temporary. He repeated the word a couple of times in his head, trying to make it stick. He'd say it a hundred times if it would help. Getting too comfortable would be a mistake he had no plans to make, no matter how much her concern for Bernie tried to penetrate the casing he'd purposely wrapped around his heart the day she ended their relationship.

Call it unfinished business, but he needed to know if his last name was the only reason for the breakup.

"Here. Let me help with that," she said, taking the end of the blanket out of his hands.

He maneuvered it underneath the dog as he slid off the bench seat. Bernie was heavy. Lucky for Jack, working a ranch was better than most personal trainers and gym memberships. Both were unnecessary to a rancher. So, carrying the large dog wasn't a problem. Carrying him in a way that didn't cause Bernie pain was another story.

With the dog in his arms, he took a step back before Natalie closed the door. As smoothly as he could, he carried the dog around the back of the house. "Can you grab the door?"

"It isn't locked?" There was shock in her voice.

"No need to out here." He'd noticed how she immediately locked the door behind them in her Austin apartment. Until recent months, Cattle Cove had always been considered a safe place to live. It was the kind of place where people left their keys in vehicles while eating in town or running inside a store. Homes were left unlocked. But the town's innocence had been shattered after it was discovered the mayor had covered up murder in order to protect his son in the decade-old deaths of a pair of preteens. Several crimes involving residents over the past few months indicated a wave that had folks eyeing strangers a little more carefully, locking doors and watching their backs.

"You always keep your doors unlocked?" She blinked at him like she couldn't believe it as she opened the door.

The question was rhetorical, so he didn't bother answering.

"What about the back door to your house?"

"Same." He walked over to the outdoor sofa and gingerly set Bernie down. "I know, buddy. We're going to get you some help."

"What can I do?" She stood there wringing her hands together.

"Go inside. Help yourself to anything you need."

She stood there, fist planted on her hip, backpack on her

back. The determined look in her eye said there was no way she was following his advice.

"Okay, fine. Get a bowl of water for Bernie." He relented, figuring this was the quickest way to get her to focus on herself. Her heart had always been soft for animals. One of her many good qualities. Not a topic he wanted to spend a lot of time on with her staying at his home. And yet, having her here felt right on so many levels.

Natalie took off and then returned in a few moments. "Here you go, sweet boy."

Bernie made quick work of the water, splashing it around as he lapped up as much as he could under the awkward circumstances.

"He's good now. You can go inside and eat," Jack urged.

After hesitating for a long moment, she relented. "Take care of him."

The reason for her reaction dawned on him. She realized she wouldn't see Bernie again, which also told Jack she planned on staying overnight tops. Good to know.

She disappeared inside as the realization punched him. The familiar ache slammed into him full force and without warning. Losing her twice was gonna be hell on his heart.

5

It was midafternoon and the sun was shining. Jack took a seat next to Bernie's head, figuring it might take Derek a little while to check on the mares. The big dog surprised him by placing his head in Jack's lap. Fleas or not, Jack didn't care. He let Bernie rest.

Surprisingly, the dog fell asleep again. He was either that tired or in that much pain. Or maybe he realized he was home. Animals surprised Jack all the time with their intuition.

At the first noise, Bernie's eyes flew open. He flinched and it reminded Jack of Natalie's reaction when he woke her.

"You're all right," he soothed, as he heard the hum of an engine pulling up beside the house. He grabbed his phone and texted his location. Derek came around the back of the house a minute later with a black bag that was very familiar. His emergency medical supplies were inside.

After giving him the rundown, Jack said, "I wish there was a way he could stay here."

Derek took a knee next to Bernie and performed a

systematic exam. "He'll be more comfortable at my office, if it makes you feel any better."

It did. Jack knew Derek would give Bernie the best care possible.

"He deserves to be comfortable," was all he could say in response.

"He'll have round-the-clock care," Derek reiterated. "And company. He won't be alone even for a second. I'll have someone from my staff inside the room with him if I can't be."

"What are we looking at here?"

"Best course of action is most likely going to be a total hip replacement. But I need to perform a complete workup and exam before any decision can be made." Derek didn't immediately stand up. "Looks like you've got yourself a good dog here."

"He deserves a real home."

"He's found that. There's no one better to take care of this guy. Let's get him healed, so he can start living his life." Derek was right. Jack was having a tough time letting go of things lately. Animals. People.

"I'll help you get him to your vehicle," he offered.

"No need." Derek hopped up and took off out the door. He returned a few minutes later with a Bernie-sized motorized gurney. "Help me get him onto this and I'll take it from here. This thing is amazing. And, don't worry. I'll head straight to my office."

Those big brown eyes weren't helping matters. Jack didn't want to leave him until the sound of a dish breaking cut through the moment.

Derek's gaze flew to the kitchen window. It was lighter outside than inside, so he couldn't see in. Luckily. He cracked a knowing smile and Jack didn't correct him. Let him believe a date had slept over.

"Let's get this big guy taken care of," Derek said. Between the two of them, they lifted Bernie with ease and placed him on the gurney. "I'll personally text updates every few hours."

"Thank you." Jack shook the vet's hand before helping him with the door. "You need a second pair of hands at your—"

"I got this," Derek said. "You go take care of your...company."

Jack nodded as he held the door open. He stood there a couple extra seconds after Derek was gone, debating whether or not he should strip his clothes off, so he didn't bring fleas in the house. An infestation was a pure pain in the backside.

And then he remembered that Natalie had gone in wearing hers. Might be too late to avoid an infestation by now. He closed the door and grabbed the blankets Bernie had been lying on a few minutes ago. The laundry room was off the kitchen, so it would be easy enough to undress there. He could throw the blankets in the wash while he was at it.

But first, he needed to see about that crash.

"Everything okay in here?" He stepped into the kitchen after toeing off his boots.

"I'm so sorry." Natalie was on the floor, picking up pieces of glass one at a time. She flashed her eyes at him, and it looked like she was holding back tears.

"Be careful. I'll be right back." He gave a wide berth as he crossed the kitchen into the adjacent laundry room. He threw the blankets into the industrial-sized washing machine along with the clothes on his back. Fortune smiled on him when he realized there was a fresh pair of boxers in the dryer. He threw those on before turning on the washing machine, scalding hot cycle, and closing the lid. He figured doubling the detergent should do the trick. And an extra hot rinse.

Then, he stopped the cycle and poked his head in the kitchen.

"I need your clothes."

"Excuse me."

"Clothes. Now. I started a load."

She blinked up at him with the most confused look on her face.

"Fleas. Remember?"

"Oh. Right. I totally forgot." She bit back a yawn. "To be honest, I didn't get any sleep last night and it's starting to show."

"Stand up carefully." She was in the thick of the broken pieces.

"Ouch." She hopped on one foot, away from the mess before she picked a piece out of the pad of her foot. She held it out on her palm. "There's one."

Jack pointed toward the sink. "Trash is in the cabinet."

She tossed it and then tip-toed over to him. "Have anything I can wear?"

He glanced around and grabbed a sheet. "Will this do until I can grab a bathrobe?"

"I can make it work." Too bad she hadn't felt the same way about the two of them. Curiosity had him wanting to know more about the guy who gave her the ring—a ring she accepted. "Can you hold it up and look the other way?"

The smile that crept across his lips wasn't his fault. And, no, he didn't need to think about her naked on the other side of the sheet he held up.

∼

NATALIE WAS KEENLY aware of how little she was wearing. She felt very exposed. An English teacher once told her there was no difference between *being* something and *being very* something. She begged to differ. Right now, she felt a *very* big difference between the two.

"What did the vet say about Bernie?" She needed to redirect her thoughts because they also wanted to remind her of just how little Jack had on, and how incredible those taut, coiled muscles had felt moving against hers at one time.

So, yeah, she was doing a great job of keeping herself in check.

But, hey, this was Jack. The best sex of her life and the guy she could admit that she'd never quite gotten over. They hadn't broken up because they didn't get along or the chemistry between them had fizzled. Those same raw emotions that had pulled her toward him in the past were still present. The reason for the breakup was the unfortunate circumstance of his celebrity last name.

And now? What did it matter? The thing she feared most happened anyway. Fontenot's people had found her. The only bright spot was that Jack had been spared. And since irony should be her middle name, she was right back where she'd started...with Jack.

"That he's most likely going to need surgery to replace the hip."

"Poor baby." She wrapped the sheet around her so tightly she couldn't breathe. Loosening the wrap, she tucked a piece of material inside the top so the whole sheet wouldn't end up unraveled at her ankles.

"He'll be so much better on the other side of surgery. I hate that he has to go through it, though." He studied her as she bit back another yawn. "Why don't you shower while I clean up in the kitchen. I'll have food on the table by the time you get back. My room is that way." He pointed toward the opposite side of the kitchen. "Take the long hallway and it's right at the end."

She was in no condition to argue. But she did need to tell him something while she had the courage. She didn't have to give away her whole story.

"Bathrobe is hanging on the back of the door. It's never been used. And there are spare toothbrushes and toothpaste in the drawer." She must've shot him a look because he added, "They're from dentist visits."

His answer shouldn't make her feel better. It was no longer her business if he was seeing anyone else. She had no right to ask, either. So, she settled on, "Thank you." Then added, "For everything today."

"No problem." He said it like it was no big deal. This was a very big deal for her. It was a foreign feeling to realize that someone had her back for a change. She'd been the only child to a single mother who'd ditched Natalie before her double-digit birthday. A visit to her grandmother's house over the summer had turned into a *See you later, alligator* moment for Natalie's mother.

Despite packing up her things the week before school started and sitting at the front door on said suitcase, waiting and excited, dear old Mom never showed. A call came two days later along with an apology and the stern advice, *Behave for your grandmother, you hear?* There was also a broken promise to pick Natalie up once her mom got settled.

Years later when her grandmother died, Natalie was on her own in the world. She had no interest in finding out what happened to her mother. That ship had sailed a long time ago and Natalie had learned to chart her own course in life. A blessing and a curse, she thought.

On the positive, there was no one around to tell her what to do. On the negative, there was no one around to help her navigate life's trickier decisions.

She looked up in time to see Jack staring at her, eyebrows drawn together. Being causal about helping someone in need must be part of the unwritten Cowboy Code. If it was, Jack had it down pat and his kindness was one of a long list of positive traits. She didn't want to let her mind go there, to remind herself what an amazing person Jack was while she'd been lying to him.

Shouldering her backpack before heading toward the hallway leading to the master suite, she stopped long enough to say, "There's no fiancé."

"Excuse me?"

"I lied to you before." She glanced toward her backpack. "And, yes, I wear a ring sometimes. It's just to ward off guys from trying to talk to me. If people think I'm married, they leave me alone. They don't ask a lot of questions or try to get to know me. It's like I'm instantly tucked into a no-fun category, which is fine with me."

His lips compressed into a thin line.

"I'm sorry." She couldn't read his expression. "Say something. Please."

"What's the real reason you push everyone away?"

"Like I said, I'm not much for talking to strangers," she admitted.

"And yet, I picked you up hitchhiking this morning."

"I wish I could explain, Jack. All I can ask is that you leave it alone. Give me a place to rest my head and I promise to leave first thing in the morning." She rubbed the goosebumps climbing up her arms.

"What if that's not good enough, Natalie?"

"Then I'll go now. Well, once my clothes come out of the wash." Her pulse kicked up a few notches and she definitely felt like she was in the hot seat. "Just give me time to regroup."

He stood there, taking her apart with his gaze.

"I don't want you to leave, Natalie. You're hungry and it's clear that you can use a hand-up. I won't force you to talk about whatever it is going on in your life, but I'd like you to consider this: if you tell me the truth, I might be able to help." His honesty struck a chord, but he had no idea what he was really asking.

She cocked her head to one side. "I am telling you the truth."

The look he shot her could melt ice in an Alaskan winter.

"I am *now*. And that's why I want to stop talking because I don't want to lie to you or misrepresent information in any way. Believe it or not, you're important to me and I don't want to do anything that could hurt you."

"It's a little late for that, don't you think?" As soon as the words came out of his mouth, he bit down on his lip like he was stopping himself from continuing. Palms out, he put his hands in the surrender position. "It's been a long day. You're hungry and tired. Let's take care of those things before we tackle anything else. Okay?"

She shouldn't agree to his statement because it implied they would continue talking about her situation later. She was done. So done. And didn't want to go there again.

Rather than stand in the man's kitchen and argue, she conceded with a small nod. No promises, though. In fact, she was too tired to form words at this point. She was also pretty sure folks in Oklahoma could smell her at this point.

Being in the vehicle with Bernie masked her scent, which had to be ripe after spending much of the night in a hot barn. Going more than twenty-four hours without a shower wasn't going to win her any points in the 'smells good' category and nothing overshadowed the scent of yesterday's coffee shop on her. As much as she loved the hot brew, she couldn't stand coffee shop smell on her clothes. Despite handing over her clothes and standing there stark naked underneath a sheet, the dark brew permeated off her skin and hair.

Padding down the hall, she was having a hard time removing Jack from her thoughts as he'd stood there and stared at her like she might've lost it. Yes, he was gorgeous. Yes, he was smart. Yes, he was funny. And, yes, he was basically everything she could ever ask for in a partner. Exactly the reason she didn't want to kill him. Being with her could be deadly.

She turned on the spigot in the shower after closing the door. People in Cattle Cove might leave their keys in vehicles and forget to lock their doors, but she was from Austin where folks locked doors inside of their houses. For example, she locked the bathroom door behind her. It was an old habit courtesy of living with roommates years ago.

Slipping out of her sheet and into the warm water of the shower was as close to heaven as she was getting tonight. She blew out a breath, more resolved than ever to stick to the plan. Shower. Eat. Rest. Leave. She repeated those words again and again in her mind until they solidified as a mantra.

6

J ack walked into his bedroom just as he heard the spigot being cut off in the bathroom. He didn't want to catch Natalie off guard, especially with the reaction she'd had in the truck on the way over. And her confession a few minutes ago about the fake fiancé caused his mind to reel.

"I'm in here," he said loud enough for her to hear through the closed door. He knew from experience the door would be locked. She'd blamed the habit on living with roommates in the past but now he wondered how much of the excuse was true.

"Okay," came the voice from the other room.

His toe caught on her backpack as he walked over to his dresser for clothes. A giant step later, he caught his balance before what would have almost certainly have been a faceplant. A painful one at that.

The backpack caught on his foot and spilled over. The zipper was open just enough for a few of its contents to spill out. He pivoted and dropped down to replace the contents, shocked at what he found.

Cash. Lots of it. Enough to make him think she'd robbed a store.

Considering the fact she didn't want to be seen, along with the fact he'd found her hitchhiking on a backroad, he surmised she must be in some kind of serious trouble. A thief? A robber? In his heart of hearts, he didn't believe either of those descriptions fit the Natalie he'd gotten to know and grown to care deeply about.

On closer inspection, all the backpack had inside it was money. On the run? A criminal?

The wedding band was in there somewhere too. Another lie. They were racking up.

An annoying voice in the back of his mind picked that moment to remind him that she'd volunteered the fake fiancé news. Being dishonest seemed to bother her enough to come clean without any prodding from him.

The irony he couldn't quite swallow came with the fact she had ended their relationship abruptly, and with very little in the way of explanation, because of a lie. Yes, she'd been upset about him misrepresenting his last name. That was on him.

But she wasn't walking out of his house without an explanation about the cash.

So, he threw on clothes, grabbed the backpack and headed to the kitchen before she came out of the bathroom.

Jack finished heating up the plates of carne asada, rice, and refried beans. He sprinkled a little extra cheese on top and added the fresh guacamole—a Miss Penny exclusive—to each plate before setting them both on the table.

Figuring the last thing Natalie needed was more caffeine, he poured her a glass of lemonade along with water for him. Since he didn't want to churn over her deception before she had a chance to explain, he redirected his focus to Bernie.

Checking his phone, he saw that a text had come through from Derek, along with a picture of Bernie looking mighty comfortable on a bed. Jack thought about the few supplies he'd need to collect from the barn for Bernie's return in what would most likely be a few days at the least. He wished the dog could come home sooner, but this way he'd have time to gather bowls, blankets and toys.

The sound of footsteps moving toward him from the hallway caused him to stop and turn around. He leaned his hip against the counter as Natalie entered the room, folding his arms.

"This smells so g—"

Her gaze landed on the chair with her backpack on display. He'd put a few stacks of bills on the table to get her attention.

"Mind telling me why you're hitchhiking through Texas with a backpack full of cash?"

"I-uh-I should probably go." She started toward the backpack at a good clip.

"First of all, I don't think you'll get far in a man's bathrobe. And, secondly, you're not getting away that easily. And before you accuse me of nosing through your personal items, I tripped over it in the bedroom."

Eyes wide, she froze. Her panic was written all over her features. She glanced around, clearly looking for the quickest exit and he could almost see her mentally debating whether she'd make it or not.

"I'm not going to force you to talk about anything you don't want to, Natalie," he conceded. "Sit down and eat. I promised you a shower, food, and a place to crash. I won't go back on my word."

She looked temporarily frozen. And then she blew out a sharp breath. "Believe me when I say that it's better if you don't know."

Her gaze locked onto the plate, but she seemed unsure if she should go for it or not.

"Go ahead. Eat while it's hot," he urged. "Everything Miss Penny makes is out of this world, but this is one of my personal favorites."

When she didn't make a move toward the dining table, he did. Once he sat down and made a show of taking a bite, she took a few tentative steps toward the table. He tipped his chin toward her chair.

She took the extra few steps as he removed the backpack and set it on the floor in between them.

Natalie eased into the chair meant for her. "This smells amazing."

"Dig in."

The first couple of bites she took slow. The next thing he knew, her plate was clear and the lemonade glass was drained. "That was beyond amazing. You weren't kidding. Miss Penny is a fantastic cook."

Pride filled his chest. Miss Penny held a spot close to his heart. He would do just about anything for the woman who had stepped in as a mother and been there for Jack, his brothers, and their cousins. "Do you want seconds?"

"If it's not too much trouble."

He got up and fixed a second helping. Then, set the plate down in front of her after heating it.

"You said it's better if I don't know what's going on with you. Would that incriminate me?" He wasn't concerned about being arrested, considering he hadn't done anything wrong.

"No."

A one-word answer wasn't his favorite.

"Would knowing put my life in jeopardy?"

She didn't look up as a red blush crawled up her neck, causing her cheeks to flush. Damned if it didn't make her even more beautiful. The fact she didn't answer meant *bingo*. He was onto something. The Natalie he knew would want to protect him.

"Is your life in jeopardy?" It was a fair question. One she gave a slight nod in response to.

Now, he was getting somewhere.

"Did you get involved in something illegal that you hadn't intended to?"

"No." She looked at him with hurt and disappointment in those gorgeous blue eyes of hers. "I didn't do anything wrong. I would never…"

She seemed to catch herself before she said too much and that shot off another warning flair. He wasn't worried about himself, but he was becoming increasingly concerned about her.

"Then, I'm at a loss here." He set his fork down. "You're obviously in some kind of trouble, but I don't know what. That makes it impossible for me to know how to help you other than to feed you, give you a chance to rest, and then let you walk out of my life forever." He paused for a moment and she didn't fill the gap with words. "Here's the thing, Natalie. I cared a lot about you once. Meaning, I didn't stop caring because you ended the relationship. And that's a problem for me because once you walk out that door, I'm not going to suddenly stop worrying about you."

She sat there, chewing the heck out of the inside of her jaw. And he could see the debate going on in her head over whether she should share more or keep quiet.

"Tell me what's going on, Natalie." He figured being

direct might help nudge her over the edge. At the rate things were going, it couldn't hurt.

"The thing is this: telling you could put you in danger. Me being here at all could put you in danger, except this place is about as secluded as it gets and so I figured it would probably be okay to stay overnight. I'm so tired and I have no idea what my next move is going to be." She sounded exhausted. "Sleep should help. And I want to feel safe again, even if it's just for one night because I haven't experienced that feeling in a very long time. Not since..."

Her voice trailed off and it was probably his bruised ego that had him wanting to fill in the sentence for her with, *being with you.*

Jack could hear the palpable loneliness in her voice. Her words were the equivalent of a gut punch. The kind that would knock the wind out of him and leave him gasping for air. His family was around at all times. Granted, he was closer to some than others as was the case in most large families, but the entire bunch was about as tightknit as it got. Without a doubt, he could count on any of his brothers or cousins to drop whatever they were doing on a moment's notice if Jack said the word. He was so used to that level of support that he was ashamed to realize he took it for granted.

Natalie had none of that support. She'd mentioned a grandmother who she'd been close to once. Best he could tell, her grandmother had already passed away. Natalie didn't speak much about her family and it had always seemed like the topic was off limits.

More jaw chewing.

"I don't know if it was coincidence or fate that brought me to you this morning but here we are. And, in case you haven't noticed, I live on a secure property that I don't leave a whole lot. If you need a place to stay for a few days, you're welcome here, Natalie. I'd prefer to know what I might be facing but you don't have to tell me anything you don't want to."

Studying her, it was obvious if she chewed on the inside of her jaw any harder, it might bleed.

NATALIE HAD to admit Jack put up a convincing argument. She searched for the right words and came up empty. Maybe she could find a way to tell him a little without giving away the whole story. Everything was happening so fast since the attempted poisoning and she needed the world to slow down for a couple of days while she got her bearings.

What if she left the ranch and then word got out that she'd been here?

Okay. Okay. There was no getting around warning him of the danger he could be in if he didn't forget about her.

"So, here's the thing. Telling you more than you already know puts you in danger."

"Believe me when I say that I don't know anything yet." He didn't back down. If anything, his gaze intensified.

"You do. You know me. You know my name." Well, that part was sort of true. He knew the name of the person she'd become. "I'm originally from a small parish outside of New Orleans."

"That's a good place to start. What else can you tell me?"

"Natalie Baker is my name. It's just not the one I was born with."

Her admission caused him to blow out a frustrated-sounding breath. His eyebrows knitted in confusion. And she could almost see the questions forming in his mind and the betrayal.

7

"Are you telling me that you were adopted or that you are married after all?"

"No. Neither of those." How much could Natalie tell him? How much could she hold back without him barraging her with questions?

"Well, then I'm confused." His eyebrows drew together.

Finding the right words was proving harder than she expected. She cared a lot about Jack. She was staying in his home, possibly putting him in danger. He deserved to know the truth and, to be honest, she wanted to be able to tell someone, to tell him. Keeping her identity a secret from everyone took a greater toll on her than she ever could've imagined it would.

The whole scenario of becoming someone else and starting a new life had sounded almost too good to be true when she'd first been approached about testifying. The federal agents on her case convinced her the Fontenots would come after her whether she did the right thing or not. Of course, she'd wanted to help bring justice on behalf of her neighbor's family when Ralph Matterson was gunned down in his driveway. Natalie had stepped outside for a morning jog, very much unlike her, and proved that she quite possibly had the worst timing in the world. She'd never been a morning person. Turned out, her neighbor was a case of mistaken identity.

The Feds had leaned on her to testify along with two other neighbors who'd stepped forward and confirmed they'd seen her outside that morning.

A part of her had mistakenly believed her old life would be easy to walk away from. It was partly true. She didn't realize how much her name was tied to her identity or how much losing it would make her feel separated from the grandmother she loved.

"I'm a singer. Or at least I was. Small town. Small time. But every time I got behind the mic and there was even one person willing to sit there and listen to me sing, it didn't feel small." She risked a glance at him as she felt her cheeks flame. "Is that weird?"

He shook his head.

"Three years ago, I witnessed a crime," she started, resigned to sharing more than she'd set out when this conversation started. He needed to know what she was up against and why it was so important not to be seen with her.

"Are you in a program?" Recognition dawned as pieces seemed to click together. A year after she moved to Austin, she'd met Jack. Straight away, she'd wanted to tell him who she really was. It was difficult to be truly intimate with someone when she had to deceive them and hide her past. Meeting him had made her realize as long as she lived a false identity, nothing in her life could be real. Renee Herbert was dead. Natalie Baker was born in her place.

"I was until I testified, and the guy was convicted," she explained.

"Game over, right?"

"Not exactly." Oh, how she wished it was that simple.

"Wait a minute. Is that why you were so obsessed with my last name?" He tilted his head back as realization dawned.

"*You* are news. I can't risk being seen and I didn't know you were famous."

"I'm not."

"I beg to differ and so does the rest of the world," she countered. "Especially those in Texas."

He conceded her point when he redirected the conversation, "But you said the trial is over. He was convicted."

"I can do you one better than that. He died in prison."

"Then I'm confused. Wouldn't that mean you could go back to your old life?" He seemed very puzzled now.

"There's no going back. And, honestly, no one to go back for. But I still can't risk my face showing up in the news. Social media is bad, but there's less chance someone will run across me under my new name. It's risky, though. An old employer or school friend could identify my face and make the connection. It's hard to stay under the radar considering how 'out there' we all are if that makes sense."

"I understand." Did he? She wanted him to. Something in his tone said he might. It wasn't much more than an undercurrent, but a steady one. Jack picked up his fork again and stabbed it into his food. "Wouldn't it be a good thing that he died in prison?"

"You'd think," she admitted. "In some ways, it probably was. But he has a son who blames me for his father's death. The government fulfilled its contract with me. I testified. We got a conviction. I got a new identity."

"One you have to protect above all else." He sounded resigned and some of the hurt had edged out of his tone.

"I do. Leaving Texas is going to be harder than I imagined. I fell in love with Austin. I'd never been there before and was surprised by the music scene. The coffee shops. The tacos."

"Austin's great. A little loud for my taste and definitely too crowded on the day-to-day. The music there can't be beat, though. And there are more young people than in Cattle Cove, that's for certain." His admission made her smile.

"Easier to go incognito for more than just witness protection people."

"I never met one person around my age in Austin who has heard of my family." There was so much relief in his voice when he said those words. She understood the burden that could come with a name. He studied her for a long moment and there was so much compassion in his eyes. "Can you go back to the marshal's service? Request a new identity?"

"I'm done with them. I didn't exactly have a great experience. Besides, I know the drill. Get a new identity and move on."

"So, I'm guessing you saw this guy's son."

She shook her head. "Not exactly."

"What happened to make you think he found you?" He quirked a brow.

"I was at the coffee shop that I used to take you to for those breakfast sandwiches," she began.

"They were made fresh." He sat up a little straighter.

"Yes, and they were so good. Although, now that I've eaten Miss Penny's cooking, I've redefined my idea of what's good." She smiled.

"But at the coffee shop...Austin..." He snapped his fingers, trying to recall the name.

"Grinds."

He nodded.

"Someone slipped poison in my coffee there."

"And you found this out how?"

"A fly of all things. You remember how the coffee shop has outside service?"

"Yes."

"It's the worst part about that place, right? Having to sit outside because there were so few seats in the dining area and..."

He looked at her to finish the sentence.

"I was studying, so I was all set up, but I needed to make a quick bathroom run. I just left everything on the table and grabbed my purse. When I come back, this fly lands in my drink and instantly dies. I picked up my cup and smelled the contents. It was different. Had a tangy, metallic smell to it. The fly instantly dropped."

"Did you call the police?"

"No. I panicked and got out of there as fast as I could. He must've seen me or been watching me, waiting for the chance. Fear kicked in and I had to move. Before I could even rationalize what I was doing, I'd cleaned out my apartment, which didn't take long. I guess I'm always preparing for something like this to happen. Always looking over my shoulder and watching my back," she admitted. It felt nice to actually be able to talk about this for a change after holding it until she could barely breathe. It was like a boulder had been docked on her chest and was finally lifting. Some of the pressure was easing and it didn't hurt to take in air.

"That's why your place was always so neat. I wondered about it. Don't get me wrong, I don't mind an orderly home, but yours always seemed extra tidy," he admitted.

"Yes. I needed to be ready to go at a moment's notice. Austin was my third city. During the trial, I got moved around a couple of times to temporary apartments. Then, came the trial and I thought life would settle down when it was all said and done. He was convicted, and I thought that since I'd done my part it would end. I naively believed I would be able to sleep at night again without every little noise causing my blood pressure to skyrocket. You know?"

"Clearly, you couldn't. And this explains what happened in the truck when I woke you up."

"That's the reason. I mean, I couldn't let my guard down after I was threatened. It took me a while, but I finally realized no one takes down a guy like Fontenot and gets off scotfree." She let out a slow breath, more of the boulder eased off her chest. "Little did I realize when this whole ordeal began that I'd end up living like a fugitive the rest of my life."

"The fly in the coffee sent you running." His voice was filled with compassion and understanding. And something that sounded a lot like concern.

"That's right. I emptied my bank account." She nodded toward the backpack. "And planned to relocate to somewhere remote, which I'm not a fan of honestly because I like city life. I think I need to really change things up this time. Go remote. Get off the grid for a while. You know?"

Jack sat there, listening. He was a good listener, nodding every once in a while to let her know he was still engaged in the conversation. His head was bowed, and she couldn't see his eyes. They usually gave away his mood. Dark and hooded, meant he was in an intense mood. Sex on those days had been hot enough to set the world on fire. Then there were his compassionate eyes—eyes that reached the depth of her soul with understanding without a word spoken between them. Bright, sparkly eyes were her favorites. Those meant an adventure waited.

When he looked up at her because she'd stopped talking, she was looking into deeply concerned eyes.

∾

"First off, we need to go to the law." Jack had no idea if he could convince her, but he had to give it a shot.

"Absolutely not." She shook her head for emphasis. "And tell them what? A fly died in my cup. I know how that sounds and I appreciate you for believing me. Most would think I'm crazy. I don't have the cup, so it's just my word at this point. And Fontenot's son will get to me if I surface again. I promise you."

It was too late to have her coffee analyzed. A dead fly and a weird smell didn't exactly qualify as attempted murder. Seemed like a backhanded way to end her life. Seriously, why come at her like that? Why not head on? Make sure that she knew before she closed her eyes for the last time her death was revenge? Why would a violent criminal organization sneak around to poison someone's drink?

"Did you see anyone familiar beforehand?" he asked.

"No. That's the scary part. It came out of the blue."

The life she'd described of always watching and waiting sounded like hell. Again, he assumed she'd overreacted about him not being straight-up about his last name. Now, he was beginning to understand why she'd be paranoid and why honesty would rank high on her list. Transparency was important to any relationship in building trust. With her, lack of it was literally a deal breaker. And then there was the incident in his truck when he had to wake her.

"Are you one hundred percent certain about what happened in the coffee shop?"

"Yes. No. Maybe." She blew out a sharp breath. "All I know for certain is that I need sleep. I've been in panic-mode for so many hours straight I can't even keep count anymore, and I'm exhausted. Can we pick this conversation up after I get some rest?"

"Yes." There was no amount of coffee in the world that could keep those sleepy eyes open. He was no longer concerned that she'd robbed a liquor or convenience store or had gotten herself into accidental trouble. He never really believed she was capable of stealing.

"This goes without saying, but I need your word that you won't breathe a word of what I've just told you." She stood up and picked up her plate.

"Don't worry about it." He followed suit, taking the plate from her hands. "I can clean up. And, no, I won't break your confidence."

For a long moment, she stood there, frozen. He almost believed he'd said something wrong but who could be offended by his offer to clean or his promise to keep her secrets?

And then she locked onto his gaze. Those cobalt blues practically pierced through him. Pushing up to her tiptoes, she pressed her lips to his.

He tensed and nearly dropped the plates because his fingers wanted to flex and release to work out some of the tension. He dipped his tongue in her mouth, remembering how sweet she tasted.

Bad idea.

This might feel like the world had just righted itself, but nothing changed between them. She was still scared of her own shadow. The kiss was most likely her needing to be reminded of life, of how good life could be.

Drawing on all his willpower, he pulled back first. She brought her hands up to his neck, tunneling her fingers in his hair. Her eyes were glittery and there was so much urgency in her touch that his pulse kicked up a few more notches.

Reminding himself to keep his feet grounded and make sure she didn't do anything she would regret; he blew out a sharp breath. "Not a good idea, Natalie. I missed you and, truth be told, I'm not over you. You've made it clear this is a pitstop for you and nothing else. So, we better keep a safe distance between us."

He surprised himself with his honesty.

Her shoulders deflated as she dropped her hands to her side. "You're probably right. For the record, I didn't want to walk away before. It's just...my life is..."

"Complicated," he finished for her. Knowing her situation helped him understand her freak out about his family's visibility.

"That's putting it lightly." Her attempt at humor failed when her smile died on her lips.

"If I really had been a random ranch worker, would it had turned out differently between us?" He couldn't help but ask. His bruised ego wanted to know if there was more to the breakup than his last name.

"Guess we'll never know," she said with a hint of melancholy in her voice.

He nodded toward the bedroom, and she took a couple of steps before stopping.

"Any chance you'll come sit with me until I fall asleep? In the truck, that was the first real sleep I've had since we..."

"I'll be right in." Jack figured there weren't many mistakes bigger than going into the bedroom with Natalie when she'd just shown her vulnerable side. And yet there he was about to make it anyway. He finished clearing the table and then rinsing the dishes before placing them inside the dishwasher.

On his way out of the kitchen, his cell buzzed, indicating he had a text. His phone was on the counter, so he backtracked and checked the screen.

Well? Your move.

The message was from Susan. She clearly expected a response, but was she still talking about the baby? He'd asked for a paternity test. There was something about the tone of her messages that made him question her mental condition.

Half the reason, check that, the *entire* reason he'd broken off their relationship was that she'd tried to get too comfortable with him way too fast. She was a prime example of the reason he stopped telling new people his real last name and never brought anyone home until he was damn certain the relationship had more than a couple of months under its belt.

Susan Fairbanks had shown up in Cattle Cove, asking around for him in town. Her car broke down on the highway and she managed to get a ride into town. Or so the story went. She was charming and, he had to give it to her, beautiful.

Rain was coming down in sheets that day. She was soaked. He broke his rule and invited her to his house. After that first night, she left behind a few personal items that he'd believed had been on accident until he caught her smirking when he asked her about them. Next thing he knew, she'd brought her favorite towel from home and hung it in the bathroom. New laundry detergent showed up, apparently her favorite.

She'd thrown an epic fit when he asked her to take her stuff home. She'd wanted to sit down and talk about where their relationship was headed. She'd caused him to second-guess his judgment about people. Prior to her, he'd believed himself to be a good judge of character.

Every now and then, a bad seed slipped through the cracks, Miss Penny had said when she'd overheard one of his conversations with Susan. She claimed a condom broke, but he would have noticed when he'd taken it off.

And, though, he didn't really believe her child belonged to him, he also realized everyone would be better off if he treaded lightly. Someone who'd proven to be off-balance emotionally wasn't someone to blow off. She needed to be let down lightly.

Hell, she might even have a baby that she believed to be his. So, he needed to come up with a game plan, and that could wait a few more hours. For now, he wanted to walk into his bedroom and...

Okay, what he *wanted* to do wasn't on the table. And, besides, it wouldn't be a good idea anyway. Losing her twice was gonna hurt like hell. Going deeper in with his emotions would only cause more pain. So, he shelved those thoughts as he navigated his way down the hallway.

"I borrowed a T-shirt and boxers. Hope that's okay." She was sitting up with the covers hiked up to her chin.

"Wouldn't be very comfortable to sleep in a robe." He smiled.

"As long as you're here, I don't think it would make a huge difference, to be honest." Those weren't the words he needed to hear because they caused his chest to squeeze and his hands to want to reach out and touch her, comfort her.

Big mistake.

Instead of falling down that rabbit hole, he positioned the chair closer to the bed, leaned back in it and kicked his feet up. A few minutes later, he heard her steady, even breathing. Sleep for him was about as far away as Canada.

No use fighting against it. He knew a losing battle when he saw one. So, he closed his eyes and pretended his heart wasn't going to break in half tomorrow after Natalie, or whatever her real name was, walked out of his life.

8

N atalie woke with a start. Her pulse raced. It was pitch black in the room. She sat up and drew the covers up to her neck as she struggled to gain her bearings.

"You're okay." Jack's low timbre reverberated through her, warming her, calming her.

"Sorry." She took in a few slow, deep breaths.

"No need to apologize." Hearing his voice again stirred up so many feelings—feelings that had her wishing she could stick around long enough to ask if he'd be willing to give their relationship a second chance. Being here with him was the first time she felt safe since the breakup.

She was still trying to figure out how Fontenot's son found her. She regretted not changing her appearance more. She'd cut off most of her hair and kept it short for the longest time after the initial threat. Growing it back had been her attempt to reclaim her life. To be *her* again after pretending to be someone else for months on end. That was the thing no one had told her before she agreed to go into protection. She would never get to be herself again.

"What time is it?" She rubbed blurry eyes.

"Quarter to four in the morning."

"Wow. I really slept."

"You needed it."

"Clearly." Her eyes hadn't quite adjusted to the dark. "Mind if I turn on a light?"

"I got it." There was a click, and then she was bathed in soft light.

"Better?" he asked.

"Much. Thank you." One look at him and she knew he was wearing the same clothes he had on yesterday. "Did you sleep like that?"

"I didn't mind."

"I'm really sorry about that—"

"You have to stop apologizing." He smiled and it warmed the room. Or, maybe, it was just her.

"I didn't mean for you to sit there this whole time." She was happy about it and figured that was the reason she'd slept so long. There he was, stretched out on a chair next to the bed.

"I nodded on and off. I've been trying to work something out in my head, and it was nice to take a minute to mull it over." Jack was devastatingly handsome. Her heart took a hit because she was going to have to walk away forever this time. "Besides, you seemed like you needed a friend."

"Anything going on that you want to talk about? I'm a decent listener." She prayed it wasn't about a relationship with another woman. Although, she'd bite the bullet and listen anyway. That was the deal once they broke up.

He shook his head.

"How'd you sleep?" He knew how to turn the tables.

"Good." She stretched out her arms and yawned,

releasing more of that pent-up tension. "Better than good actually. I slept great."

"How about some coffee?"

"Sounds like heaven to me." The time would come in a couple of hours for her to gather up her things and take off. Now, she wanted to spend a little while with the man she knew, without a doubt, she would never forget.

Jack stood and stretched out his arms. The cotton of his shirt stretched and released, revealing layers of taut muscles. Since no good could come from her staring at her ex-boyfriend's chest, she forced her gaze away.

The man was physical perfection. She didn't need to be reminded of the fact.

Once he left the room and disappeared into the bathroom, she threw off the covers and located the robe. Her clothes should be clean and dry by now, so she could change into those in a minute. After coffee.

As soon as the sink water turned off in the next room, she was ready for her turn. He opened the door to find her standing there, practically bouncing on one leg.

"All yours." He stepped aside and smiled.

A few minutes later, she headed into the kitchen refreshed. It was amazing what a good night of sleep could do for a person's overall outlook. That, and the fact she felt safe for the first time in too long.

"Are you hungry?" Jack handed her a cup of coffee.

She took a sip, enjoying the burn on her throat. "I could eat something simple, like yogurt. Don't go to any more trouble than you already have."

He smiled again, and it was devastating.

She turned toward the table as he moved in the direction of the fridge. "This coffee is amazing."

"Pods make it easy. I promise no one will ever accuse me

of being a genius in the kitchen." He set down a yogurt container along with a spoon.

"Do you eat breakfast?"

"Not before my first cup of coffee." He took a seat at the table and she noticed he had his cell phone in his hand. He studied the screen.

"Everything okay?"

"A former friend of mine is distressed and I'm not sure what I can do to help." The slight emphasis he put on the word *friend* told her this was someone he'd dated. Jealousy ripped through her, targeting the center of her chest and making it hard to breathe.

"Do you always go around saving women in trouble?" she teased, needing a light-hearted start to the day that would, no doubt, become heavier the longer she was awake. She needed to make a big decision this morning. Next move. Rent a remote cabin somewhere off the grid? Move to a major city? One of the Dakotas? Move out West?

"Only on my days off from the ranch." He winked and a dozen butterflies released in her stomach. He was playing the light-hearted game along with her, but the serious lines cutting into his forehead told her that his thoughts were preoccupied.

"Anything I can help you with? I'm pretty good at solving other people's problems, just not my own." She ran her finger along the rim of her coffee cup before picking it up and taking another sip.

"You have enough going on without trying to solve my problems." Again, she had a reaction to feeling shut out of his life.

"I don't mind, Jack. Really. Take me up on my offer. Sometimes it helps to get a fresh perspective."

He studied her for a long moment. Took a sip of coffee. Set his cup down.

"I've been receiving texts and e-mails from an ex who says I fathered a child. The kid is five-months-old."

"Does this person live here in Cattle Cove?"

"Austin."

"Oh. Is that what you were doing there when you found me?"

"Partly. I volunteered to be the one to go down and pick up the mares because I wanted to swing by and see the kid."

"So, this kid *might* actually be yours?" She couldn't believe he'd be careless.

"The dates match up to when I dated her mother," he admitted. "But, no, I don't think she's mine."

"You're concerned about her, though," she surmised.

"There's something very off with Susan." His lips thinned when he mentioned her name. "That's my ex's name."

"You said the kid was five months old. Why come after you now?"

"That was my first question." He picked up his phone. "She's been texting. Making demands. I thought I could go to Austin, get a look at the kid, maybe assess the situation and reason with the mother. Not have to get lawyers involved. Make sure the kiddo was okay."

"Does this sort of thing happen to you a lot?"

"Enough to make me leery of giving out my last name to new people," he admitted.

Her mouth formed an O but no sound came out.

"For what it's worth, I wanted to tell you my real last name. I was just waiting for the right time and, honestly..." He paused for a long moment, looking like he was debating telling her the rest. "I held off because I realized how much you valued honesty and I thought I'd lose you."

JACK HAD CALLED that one correctly. He wasn't much of a betting man, but he would've bet the farm on that one. And he would have been right.

"It didn't help your case that I found out on my own," she admitted.

"How did you, by the way?" He never did find out what had tipped her off.

"I caught on while we were out to dinner. The people at the booth next to us recognized you. Then, I heard waitresses whispering about you. The funny thing about it is that I thought you always used cash, at least when I was around, because you had bad credit."

They both laughed at that one.

"Yeah. Credit's not really a problem for me. Cash ensures no one thanks me using my last name," he admitted. "Plus, I mainly use credit to keep track of my gas records. Most of my drives to Austin are business-related."

"The other crazy thing is that you had your wallet at my house next to your keys in the bowl next to the door. You just tossed them both in every time you came over. The evidence was there the entire time. Right under my nose. If I'd opened your wallet one time, you would have been caught." She shook her head.

Jack's cell buzzed. He checked the screen. It was A.J., one of his brothers. "Everything okay?"

"Yes," A.J. started. "I'm wondering where you are, though."

"Oh. Right. I was supposed to run fences with you today.

Forgot. That's on me. In fact, I need to take another trip to Austin, so I won't be able to help out today."

"More animals?"

"Something I have to check on down there." Jack wouldn't lie to his brother, but he didn't have to go into details, either.

"But you're otherwise all right?" A.J. asked. Everyone had been checking on each other a little bit more ever since their dad's accident. It was the reminder they needed that time was guaranteed to no one. It had made everyone a little nicer to each other. It had made everyone slow down and spend more time together.

"All good here. You?"

"Better now," A.J. said. "I'll check in with you later. Make sure you're doing okay."

"Sounds good. Don't count on me today or tomorrow, though," he said.

"Gotcha."

"Any word on Dad?"

"Still no memory of what happened. He's doing great, though. He's already tired of being in the hospital and Miss Penny is getting everything set up for him to come home," A.J. said.

"And when will that be?"

"Tonight, if Dad has his way." A.J. laughed and it broke up some of the tension of the call.

"Sounds like he's on the road to recovery," Jack agreed.

"You know Dad. He's about as patient as a bull in front of a red blanket."

"Truer words have never been spoken." Their father was infamous for his ability to dig his heels in and stand his ground. He was smart enough to know which issues warranted it. "It's good to hear that he sounds like his old self again."

"What do you think about Uncle Donny's arrest?"

"Probably the same as everyone else. I don't want it to be true, but that doesn't necessarily mean that I don't believe it's possible." Their uncle had abandoned his children, leaving their father to raise them as his own. Personally, Jack didn't have a problem with it. He loved his cousins as though they were siblings. Growing up with a big family, all of whom had his back, had made for a near-perfect childhood. And since no one was actually perfect, not even their dad, Jack had another question. "Has Dad mentioned anything that might clear up Kurt's situation?"

"Only that he wanted us to welcome Kurt into the family."

"Did someone mention that already happened?"

"You know it. Levi mentioned it, but, damn, that's a tricky one to talk to the old man about." A.J. blew out a sharp breath. "Dad asked everyone to make an appearance at Sunday supper. Said he had a few announcements to make."

"And you're thinking one of those announcements will help us understand why he cheated on Mom?" Their mother had been planning a pre-kindergarten party for A.J. when her life had been cut short while out on an errand. It wasn't like they could bypass their dad on this one. By all accounts, his parents had loved each other deeply. So, Jack and the others were scratching their heads as to why the man would have cheated on her. Obviously, the wound was still raw.

They didn't blame Kurt. He'd fought harder against becoming a McGannon than they'd expected. He wasn't there for money or opportunity. He ran a successful logistics business that he'd grown from the ground up. His wife had died after childbirth. He had an adorable little girl. Uncle Donny had been the one to contact him, stirring up the pot in a way only their uncle could.

That part of Donny's personality was the reason they couldn't rule him out as a suspect. As much as they wanted to and felt like they were betraying their cousins, they couldn't put it past Donny. And that was just sad. Family was everything to a McGannon. But there were two sides forming in the *he did it,* or *he didn't do it* debate. Dividing the family and creating two distinct schools of thought.

Not that Jack blamed his cousins for wanting to believe in their father. He was a little surprised they couldn't see through the man who'd abandoned them after asking to cash out his inheritance of the family cattle ranch. Then there was the issue of how he'd blown the money and that he'd done so in record time. Gambling. Coming back for another hand-out made him even less popular.

Jack's father was a saint for taking his brother in and giving him a place of respect in the family. Jack knew, without a doubt, his father had done it for Donny's sons.

"I have no answers there," A.J. admitted.

"Give Dad a hug for me? Tell him I'll be there on Sunday."

"You do realize today's Friday, right?"

"I got it."

"Almost forgot. Have you had your cell on you lately?"

"Yeah, why?" His service could usually be counted on at his house but there were times his connection could be iffy depending on where he was standing.

"Security said you got a package and they couldn't get a hold of you. Some hand-delivered something or other. A woman stopped by last night. Got upset when they wouldn't let her in. Said she had a present for you, but you weren't returning her texts. She said it was urgent you receive this package right away."

"I'll give 'em a call." Didn't that send a chill racing down his back.

"Declan swore he saw someone in the truck with you yesterday. Everything all good?"

"I have company."

"Oh. Oh. I better let you go then." A.J.'s awkwardness would have been funny under different circumstances.

Except that Jack hadn't been as sly as he thought, Susan was in the area, and Natalie's eyes were wide open as she listened.

A sinister thought struck. What if Susan had snapped and there was a dead baby in the box? Jesus, he didn't want to go there. Not even hypothetically. But he needed to be ready for anything and that was the absolute worst-case scenario for him.

9

"I'll have security bring the package here." Jack ended the call with his brother. He fired off a text, and then turned his attention back to Natalie.

"What do you think is going to be in there?" Her wide eyes said she caught onto his concern.

"We'll know when it arrives." He issued a sharp breath. "I can't help but think I should've done something before now. She's been crying for help with those texts. I should have figured out a way to help her."

"Are you one hundred percent certain there is a child? Someone dealing with their own mental health might not exactly be honest, through no fault of their own."

"Fair point. The thing is, she was incredibly pushy and clingy when we dated, which was short-term, but she seemed normal otherwise. Just like she wanted attention a little too much and needed love to be validated." He certainly didn't think she'd fixate on him to the degree she had. But then, things had been quiet for a long time.

"How'd she take the break-up news when you ended the relationship?"

"Hard." He stabbed his fingers in his hair before taking a lap around the kitchen. "You know how it is. I work long hours and don't have cell coverage half the time when I'm on property. It's not like I can always get right back to someone who calls or texts while I'm working."

She nodded.

"Susan flipped out. I just chalked the whole episode up as hurting. She threw out a few threats, but I highly doubt she meant them. I still don't. I doubt she even remembers what she said. You know how someone can get in the heat of the moment."

"Break-ups aren't easy to deal with," she admitted.

He put his hand out, palms up. "The person I knew wouldn't do anything irrational. Leave a few tipsy voice-mails...maybe. Have a slighter harder time letting go...yes. The texts she's been sending me lately don't sound like her at all. I know almost a year and a half has passed since we dated, but could anyone really change to that degree?"

"Something might have happened to her to trigger an over-the-top response," she hedged.

"That's what worries me."

"But the possibility the child is yours exists?" Natalie asked again.

"Afraid so." What could he say? They'd had sex. Protected. Condom. Every time. He'd liked Susan and enjoyed spending time with her early on. She'd shown her true colors and he'd shown her the way out. She'd taken it harder than was comfortable, but then when was a break-up ever pleasant?

"How long have you known about this?" Natalie's face was unreadable.

"Just found out recently," he admitted.

"Did you ask for a paternity test?"

"No, not at first. I blew off the accusation at first, thinking it would go away. I had no reason to believe I'd fathered a child. I'm careful. *This* type of incident is the exact reason I protect my name. One minute, I'm getting to know someone and, I think, having a great time. The next, she's suing for paternity or telling me news stories she'd read about my family growing up. Or she knows all my brothers' names almost better than I do. It's not just creepy, it feels invasive and criminal."

Jack expected to see fire in Natalie's eyes when he looked at her. He didn't. Instead, there was compassion and maybe a little bit of guilt.

"Life can be crazy at times," she said. Exactly the reason he believed finding happiness with someone was worth holding onto.

But he needed to change the subject. Distract himself from worst-case thinking about Susan and the possible child. "Between the two of us, we're a pair. I'm sorry any of this is happening to you, by the way. You don't deserve it. I do finally understand why you didn't tell me about your situation before. And yet, part of me thinks I could have helped."

"That's exactly the reason, Jack. You're that guy who would end up hurt or dead in a situation like this. I couldn't...*can't*...do that to you. I thought you were some random guy nobody knew when we first dated. I thought I could fly under the radar with you. You know?"

"Yes." There were days when he did, too.

"You have a big last name. One that gets attention and that's something we both know I can't afford." He knew all about the downside that came along with a prominent last name. She waved her hand in the air at the same time his phone dinged.

"I'd like to continue this discussion when we have time to really talk about it." He locked gazes with her. "The package just arrived."

She stood up, bounced was more like it, and followed him to the front door. She was careful not to be seen by security, who was currently driving away.

Jack waved and then stared at the box. It was the size of one of those old-fashioned hat boxes that Jack imagined one of his grandmothers might have owned. He nudged it with his toe, and nothing inside moved or made noise. No doubt a good sign. He was able to exhale a little as he picked it up. The box wasn't heavy, didn't tick and there was no weird smell. More good signs.

He brought it inside the house and into the kitchen where he set it on the countertop. He poked the nondescript brown box a few more times just to be sure. Nothing happened.

He lifted the lid slowly. Still nothing. Except for a whole lot of tissue paper. He moved it aside to reveal a pink baby booty that looked handmade. Crochet.

Underneath the baby booty was a note that read:

I won't be ignored, Jack. I don't care what I have to do. We belong together.

Eternally yours,

Susan

As far as creepy notes went, this one was right up there. A cold chill raced up his spine while reading it.

"I have to go see her. Talk some sense into her. Assess whether or not the baby is okay."

◦

"BAD IDEA, JACK."

Natalie didn't know Susan personally, but this note was a veiled threat if ever there was one.

"What if I can help?" His tone was a mix of torment and frustration.

"What if seeing you makes matters worse?" She walked over and locked the front door before urging him back into the kitchen. "It would probably be a good idea to bring law enforcement in at this point."

He shook his head.

"As far as I know, it's not illegal to send a few texts and drop off a 'present' for an ex."

"She needs a wellness check or something. Maybe bring in Austin P.D. I know they'll perform them if there's cause to think someone might be in danger."

"She dropped off the package here. Besides, I don't even know if she lives in the same building as when we dated. I haven't kept up with her."

"You have a last known address. What about calling in an investigator? Do you know anyone who could track down the information on her? Confirm she had a child in the timeframe she stated? You have to consider the fact she could be lying about a pregnancy. In a worst-case scenario, she could have stolen someone's child. We don't know the first thing about where she lives or what she's doing."

Jack tilted his head slightly to one side as he made a fresh cup of coffee and handed it to her. He made a second one for himself.

Since she took his silence to mean he was actually hearing her out, she continued, "If she has escalated her... whatever *this* is...fantasy...to the next level, I doubt she'll walk away at this point until she's made her point."

"What can she possibly have to gain from this?" He

motioned toward the box he'd brought into the kitchen and set on the counter.

"Real or imagined, there's a baby. She has convinced herself that you're the father. In a twisted way, she might think the three of you could be a family." She took a sip of coffee. "She might have been in a relationship for all we know and then snapped after he left. She could've reverted in her thinking to the last person she dated. You."

"You're right. I need to get someone on the case." Jack took another lap around the kitchen. The look on his face when he stopped was a knife to the chest. "Where does that leave us?"

"Believe me when I say that I want to be here for you right now," she started.

"But?" The same brow arched, and she instantly knew what he was thinking.

Why did there always have to be a 'but?' He was right, though. "All I will do is bring more confusion and sadness to your doorstep."

Jack's cell buzzed, cutting into the moment. He glanced at the screen. "It's Derek."

Natalie exhaled, listened as he took the call. It was short. After saying a few uh-huhs into the phone, he set the phone down.

"Derek thinks it's a good idea for me to visit Bernie. How do you feel about coming along?"

"I'd like that a lot." She wanted to see the sweet dog one more time before she headed out for her next stop, wherever that was going to be. "But first, will you make the call to Austin P.D., or do you want me to?"

"I'll do it." Jack issued a sharp sigh.

She helped him look up the non-emergency number and sat quietly as he conveyed his concerns for one of the town's residents. He gave as much information as he had available to him, which was basically limited to her name and last known address as well as her employer.

"We'll see what we can do," the dispatcher's tone came across as hopeful. "Can I call you back at this number?"

"Please do." Jack didn't sound one hundred percent certain this was a good idea, but he'd gone along with it and she appreciated him for the trust. Trust. Was it weird that he was basically the only person on earth she trusted? Or maybe a better question was this...was it weird that she was prepared to walk away from the only person she trusted and never look back? Because that's exactly what she had to do at some point today, no matter how much the thought made her stomach churn and her heart squeeze.

"And, sir. If she contacts you again, you might want to refrain from answering."

Didn't those words send a cold chill racing down Natalie's back.

"Will do." Jack issued a sharp sigh after ending the call. He caught Natalie's gaze. "She could be anywhere."

"True." She seemed to be escalating. "We'll have to be very careful on the way to the vet's office. It's possible she's still in the area."

Jack held up his index finger before excusing himself and moving out of the room. When he came back, he produced a baseball cap and a scarf. "Miss Penny makes a new scarf every year at Christmas. Might as well put it to use. Living in Texas, we don't have a whole lot of need for them. It should hide some of your face." She was almost certain she'd heard him whisper *shame* and that inconvenient blush crawled up her neck at the compliment. She'd never been stellar at hiding her body's reaction to Jack.

"Do you still keep a pair of sunglasses in your Jeep?" she asked, refocusing.

"Right. Yes. Those will help, too. We'll be better off taking the pickup since my Jeep is distinct." The realization Susan would know his personal vehicle wasn't exactly warm and fuzzy. Thinking about his ex wasn't the greatest thing, either. But they were adults. She had a past. He had a past. The realization struck.

"It'll be good for your family and staff not to be able to give a description of me," she pointed out.

"You might be surprised at their ability to keep a secret." The slight mix of hurt and disappointment in his tone was a knife to the chest.

Rather than acknowledge it or dwell on it, she forced a smile and wrapped the scarf around her neck.

"I can't wait to see how Bernie's doing," she said.

10

——————

"Hey, Bernie." Seeing the big dog hooked up to an IV, monitors beeping low and steady in the background, wasn't warm and fuzzy for Jack. He'd spent more time in a hospital following his father's accident than he cared to for the rest of his life. This seemed like a good time to remind himself that his new buddy would be fixed up and coming home to heal in no time. Jack was already mentally calculating the number of treats this guy was going to be getting once he came through surgery with flying colors.

The earlier conversation with Natalie edged in Jack's thoughts. She would be leaving soon. The reminder seemed necessary, considering his heart seemed to have a mind of its own. It had him wanting to pick up where they left off before the last name reveal.

Bernie perked up as Jack walked closer. The dog's eyes were brighter. Signs of life were a good thing.

"He looks so much better already," Natalie said, following closely behind Jack. "It looks like he's been given a bath. His fur looks so soft and his markings are so beautiful."

"He's a good boy." Jack had noticed how shiny Bernie's coat was.

Natalie moved beside Jack. Her cobalt blue eyes were wide, rimmed with the thickest set of black eyelashes, bringing out more of that brilliant night-sky color.

"This is already a vast improvement over what he looked like before." With Natalie standing next to him and her flowery scent filling his senses, his voice was a little huskier than he'd intended.

Thankfully, Derek knocked on the opened door and then entered the room.

"That tells me I'm doing my job well." Derek smiled. He shook Jack's outstretched hand before shaking Natalie's. "He came in suffering from severe dehydration."

"Was that the cause for his listlessness?" Jack asked, figuring as much.

"A big part. He'd been fed okay, if not well, for the most part. He came in hungry and it looked like he'd missed a few meals, so that compounded the dehydration," Derek continued.

Natalie leaned in and hugged the animal and when she glanced up, her eyes were red-rimmed. Not exactly helping Jack keep his feelings in check, but Bernie deserved that and so much more.

"His coat is gorgeous." Natalie scratched Bernie behind the ears. If he'd been a kitten, he would have purred.

Again, Derek smiled. "No more fleas, either. Which has made him a whole lot more comfortable. He'd scratched a couple of places bald, but I gave him relief from those hotspots."

"What else?" Jack wanted the whole picture and he could see there was more in Derek's eyes.

"He tested heartworm positive."

Not a shock, but it did make Jack ball his fists at his sides. He reminded himself to breathe.

"Which is another item on the punch list. I've already started his medication," Derek reassured.

"How long until he can come home?" The faster, the better in Jack's estimation. Bernie was about to be spoiled big time. Never again would he be left outside in the heat. Never again would he be denied food and water. Never again would he be left to his own devices or neglected.

"There's some good news to share on the pre-op. Based on his X-rays, I'll be able to reshape and reorient the acetabulum and femur so that the two joint surfaces are in a more normal position with minimal surgical impact." Derek checked in with Jack.

"Sounds promising."

"I'll need to keep him here for at least a day after surgery. It's looking more like two, but I'll know better once the procedure is complete." Derek spoke mostly in laymen's terms. "I'm going to recommend the full twelve-week recovery period be adhered to for proper healing. You know me, I'm always going to err on the side of caution."

"What can I do to start getting ready for him at home?" Jack nodded. He'd always appreciated that about Derek. He respected the animals, and his care was topnotch. The term *going above and beyond* most definitely applied here. And as much as Jack would like to take Bernie home to let the spoiling begin, he would heed the medical advice from their family friend. Jack trusted Derek's advice.

"You'll need to be prepared to limit his movement. Might

be best to use some type of enclosure," Derek said. "Once he starts feeling better, he won't like it."

"I can rearrange some of my responsibilities at the ranch to make sure I'm with him as much as possible. When I can't be home, I'll have someone come sit with him." Jack's family could be counted on to pitch in. "If he has company, he'll go less stir crazy."

"His size will help. He seems to be a sweet, docile animal. Once he's recovered, we'll talk about exercise, which you'll likely have to prod him to do until he gets used to it. Given the poor condition of his muscles, he was probably chained to that porch most of his life."

Jack took in a deep breath rather than release the string of expletives that came to mind. He flexed and released his fingers a few times to work out some of the tension building. This seemed like a good time to remind himself Bernie's life had just changed for the better. Since Jack couldn't go back and undo the past, he did his level best to focus on today, and where to move forward from here.

"How old is he?" Jack asked.

"Somewhere between three and four years old," Derek said.

He watched as Natalie moved to Bernie's side. The big guy's tail started working double time. It warmed Jack's heart to see the two of them together and one word came to mind...*home.* A bolt of stray lightning struck his chest and for a split second all he heard was ringing in his ears. His mind, on the other hand, was crystal clear in what it wanted.

It was wholly unfortunate. If the two had met at a different time in her life and at a different place, they might have had a chance. They, hopefully, could've gotten past the last name snafu. She said she understood his reasoning after learning about the paternity accusation. Or, should he say *accusations*? As long as he'd been dating there were people coming out of the woodwork.

Lately, and he figured it was because he'd locked in with Natalie for a time, the number of cases dropped. He heaved a sigh. But there would always be people trying to lay claim.

People on the outside figured having money solved all problems. Jack could personally vouch for the fact that having large sums of money brought its own set of troubles. No one was immune to suffering. No one got a free pass when it came to life's disappointments. No one got to cherry pick. Life was equal parts bad and good.

Having money didn't change the natural order. Where it did help was being able to provide the best possible care for the animals Jack loved.

"A couple more days, Bernie. Hang in there a couple more days for me."

"Did you see that?" Natalie asked.

Jack nodded. He could've sworn Bernie smiled.

"Mind if we stick around with him for a little while?" Jack asked Derek.

"Not at all." Derek tucked his clipboard underneath his arm and walked into the adjacent office. He paused at the door. "I'll close this to give you some privacy."

"Thank you," Jack said.

"If you have any questions, you know my cell number."

Jack nodded.

"You're such a good boy," Natalie said to Bernie. "He's so soft now. Did you feel his fur?"

"I sure did. It's so much better than the matted fur from yesterday. Texas summers will be tricky for him as thick as it is, but we'll get it figured out."

"True. Maybe give him a summer shave," she said,

scooting the rolling chair closer so she could sit near his head. "I bet you'd like that, wouldn't you?"

"What do *you* think about him and me?" The question came out before he had time to reel it in.

"Together?" She blinked at him, looking a little confused. "Perfection. I think you guys were made for each other."

"I think he'll fit in at the ranch just fine," he agreed, redirecting his thoughts from the one question he wanted to ask. *What did she think about giving him a second chance?*

Good question. Bad timing. And since he liked rejection about as much as he liked drinking vinegar straight from the bottle, he decided to keep his cards close to his chest for now. There was something stirring inside him since seeing her again, an unease, a feeling of ache or regret. He couldn't exactly pinpoint it. Until he knew exactly what he was dealing with, he decided to leave it alone for the time being.

Besides, what good could come of being rejected twice?

NATALIE SNUGGLED AGAINST BERNIE. The thought of this sweet boy needing surgery practically gutted her. She hated the idea he might be in any pain. Of course, now, he was sitting pretty.

"Hi, sweetheart," she soothed. "All of this is going to be a bad dream soon enough and you'll be on the road to healing."

Jack pulled up a chair beside hers and her heart dove off a cliff. The freefalling sensation low in her stomach was both exciting and scary. Wasn't that the best way to describe love?

Love?

As much as she didn't want to go there with anyone, she couldn't deny her feelings for Jack ran deeper than anything she'd ever experienced. Was it wrong that before him not one man she'd dated stirred her heart or caused those runaway butterflies in her stomach?

But her life was complicated. Her life didn't include white picket fences or husbands with famous last names. Her life didn't magically work out.

So, she refocused on Bernie.

"Can we come see him again tomorrow?" she asked, knowing full well she was leaving today. Wishful thinking?

"He'd like that. Wouldn't you, Bernie?" Jack scratched the dog behind the ears and she could've sworn the animal smiled for the second time.

"I'm pretty sure that you're his favorite person right now."

Jack wiggled his eyebrows and it made her laugh. She couldn't help it. She loved when Jack was being silly, corny, and pretty much every other mood. "I may have figured out the magic spot." He laughed when Bernie's leg started scratching empty air.

Without debating it, Natalie leaned in and kissed Jack. Probably a mistake considering how attracted she still was to him. Figuring that wasn't going away anytime soon and tired of fighting against what her heart wanted, she leaned into the feeling a little more.

It didn't take long for his tongue to thrust into her mouth and her to welcome his taste. There was still a hint of coffee on his lips. Dark roast was her new favorite flavor. Before she could get too carried away, she pulled back.

As they tried to catch their breath, the door opened.

"Oh. Sorry. Wrong room." The tech's voice was the equivalent of a bucket of ice water poured over her head.

Reality served cold and hard.

"No problem." There was more than a hint of embarrassment in Jack's voice no matter how cool he tried to play it.

The door closed but Natalie could almost hear the tech smiling. Busted. Big time. She looked at Jack.

"Guess we weren't as slick as we thought we were being," she said.

"It's a little too easy to get lost in the moment with you."

She wasn't sure if that was a good or bad thing. She'd take it as a good thing. Until a little voice in the back of her head reminded her it could be a dangerous thing. Get distracted at the wrong moment and Roch Fontenot could capitalize on the mistake.

Being here with Jack and Bernie was the closest she'd felt to home in too long. But then, being anywhere with Jack gave her the same feeling. Right guy. Wrong time.

Letting her imagination run wild into territory like... what would it be like if she tried to stick around town?...was counterproductive and would only lead to more heartache. "Are you ready to go home?"

His eyes lit up when she spoke the last word, releasing a dozen butterflies in her chest. Her stomach launched into one incredible somersault routine, as well. So, great, she was handling herself *really* well when it came to containing her emotions with Jack.

But, hey, if there was a person worth busting through boundaries with, it would be him.

"I'll see you tomorrow. Later today, if I can talk Derek into it," Jack whispered to Bernie. For the third time during their short visit, she could've sworn the animal smiled. But then, animal didn't seem like the right word to describe Bernie. He had that 'old soul' quality, wise beyond his years.

Jack started for the door to the lobby and she took the opportunity to lean in close to Bernie's ear and say, "Hey fella. I might be gone by the time you get out of here but that doesn't mean you won't hold a special place in my heart for the rest of my life."

Surprising tears sprang to her eyes as she kissed his forehead. His shiny coat radiant and dignified. All the knots were gone, and he smelled like a mix of lemons and sunshine.

"Be good for Jack. Okay, Bernie?"

Natalie couldn't pinpoint the exact reason walking out of that room and away from Bernie threatened to buckle her knees. An overwhelming sadness blanketed her, making it difficult to breathe. She might have said she'd be back tomorrow but she had no plans to be in Cattle Cove.

If Jack noticed the tears, he didn't say a word about them. He just reached for her hand and then linked their fingers as they crossed the lobby and moved toward his truck. At the vehicle, he stopped and pulled her into a hug. He whispered quiet reassurances into her ear as he stroked her hair with long, rough fingers.

She pushed up to her tiptoes, locked gazes with him, and then pressed a kiss to his lips. Soft at first, it gave way to passion in a matter of a few breaths. There was something urgent and different about this kiss—different than any in their past or since fate had reunited them.

Two words came to mind, *Game changer.*

When his tongue dipped inside her mouth, her knees literally weakened. She brought her hands up to grip his chest, using her fingers to trace the hard lines, memorizing every inch of him. His skin was silk over steel.

His hands cupped her face, positioning her for better

access as he deepened the kiss. Breath ragged, heart pounding, she pressed her body flush with his.

One of his hands dropped to the small of her back where it splayed. It didn't take much urging to pull him toward her until her back flattened against the hard surface of the truck.

The sound of a vehicle on the nearby roadway caused them to break apart sooner than either wanted. The car was a reality check. They were out in the open. Anyone could drive past even though the road was two-lane and out in the sticks. They needed to cool it. So, they stood there, breathing in and out like they'd just finished a hard run.

And then Jack's face broke into a wide smile in a show of perfectly white, perfectly straight teeth.

"I missed you, Natalie."

Of course she would run into the one person she couldn't forget and, honestly, didn't really want to. Murphy's Law.

11

"We should probably get out of here." One look into Natalie's eyes and Jack knew she was starting to say her goodbye to Bernie. Jack's heart literally felt ripped out of his chest.

"Okay." The one word, spoke with such resignation, confirmed what he already knew.

This time would be different, he tried to argue. His heart called BS. She wasn't walking away because the relationship had run its course or because she didn't care about him anymore. This was purely out of necessity, at least in her mind. She was trying to protect him by leaving.

He climbed into the driver's seat, chewing on those thoughts as he made the half hour drive back to the ranch. He parked and the minute he stepped out of the vehicle, he felt a wall come up between him and Natalie.

She walked into the house in front of him and straight to the kitchen table where her backpack had been tucked underneath a chair.

His cell buzzed, so he fished it out of his front pocket.

You called the cops on me?????

"What is it?" Natalie's tone mirrored his level of concern. "Another text."

She moved beside him and checked out the screen. "That's not the same number she used before."

"No, it isn't." Not a good sign. He thought about what the dispatcher had said about not responding. His fingers itched to shoot back a note. To see if he could find out what was really going on and why she suddenly wanted to tell him that he was a father. She'd gone through an entire pregnancy, birth, and five months had passed. Why get ahold of him now? And why the desperation?

His cell rang in his hand while he was still holding it. Natalie jumped and gasped. Her hand came up to cover her heart as both of their pulses jacked up.

Another unknown caller. Dispatch?

"Are you going to answer that?" she asked.

"Better let it run into voicemail just in case it's her. Based on the tone of her text, I doubt this would be a good time to have a conversation no matter how frustrating this is." And that was just the thing. Jack wasn't used to being passive when an issue arose. When there was a problem on the ranch or in his personal life, he dealt with it head-on. None of this waiting nonsense. And yet, he could acknowledge this was different. At the ranch, he sometimes dealt with strong, conflicting opinions. A mental breakdown—and he was just guessing here, but it was on the table considering her actions—was a whole different ballgame. One he had no experience with, so it was best to sit on the sidelines despite a deep-seated desire to roll up his sleeves and work until the problem was solved.

"I know you want to help and sometimes the best thing you can do is nothing," Natalie broke through his thoughts.

"I guess." He walked over and set the phone down on

the table, waiting for the voicemail notification. In the meantime, he decided to turn the tables on Natalie. "Where are you headed to now?"

Crossing the room in a few steps, she didn't make eye contact. Instead, she took a seat at the table and ran her finger along the markings in the wood. Her lips were sealed. The reason took a second to dawn on him.

"Right. You can't have anyone knowing your new location," he stated the obvious.

She nodded her head in response and didn't look up to meet his gaze.

The voicemail notification popped up on his phone, breaking the tension that had suddenly made the air feel like July in New Orleans. Too thick to breathe. He put the replay on speaker and the dispatcher's voice came on the line. "Sir, we were unable to confirm wellness for Ms. Fairbanks. Her landlord said she hasn't been back to her apartment in several days. We will continue to monitor the situation. Thank you for calling."

"At least it's confirmed she still lives at the same apartment as before," Natalie said. "Where did you say she worked?"

"A popular barbecue place on 11th Street," he said.

"I know where you're talking about. Can't remember the name, though." She groaned, looking relieved to be talking about anything but her situation. "But the lines are the stuff legends are made of. It's worth the wait, though. Really great food."

"I could give them a call to see if she still works there." The odds probably weren't in his favor, but he was willing to give it a shot.

"Would it be better if I made the call?" She made eyes at him. "You know, seem less like you're trying to check up on her. She seems pretty upset that you called the police for a wellness check and she has no idea who I am. I could pretend to be an old friend. Or, better yet, I could say I'm asking for a reference to verify employment for a new apartment."

He nodded. "Also leads me to believe she is back in the area. The landlord might not have seen her, but she has to be nearby to know about the cops."

"Her landlord could have left a message on her voicemail. He might be concerned about her," she reasoned.

"True."

"I'll call using my phone. I have to ditch it later today anyway and it'll make it impossible to trace the call back to you." She reached into her backpack and produced a cell. So many deceptions. And yet, Jack felt like he knew all the really important things about her. He felt like he knew the real person underneath the fake name and protective layers she'd built over the years. He'd seen her stripped down and vulnerable. Her strength amazed him. There was always so much brewing behind those cobalt blue eyes of hers and she almost always looked like she had a story to tell.

He didn't know the half of it when they'd dated months ago.

Natalie made the call to the barbecue house after he looked up the number on his phone. She put the call on speaker.

"This is Emeline. How can I help you?" a young, chipper voice asked. Austin teemed with college kids and she sounded par for the course.

"Hi, my name is Amelia and I'm calling to verify employment on one of your employees." She sounded every bit the part.

"My manager isn't available right now, but I can have him call you back," Emeline said.

"Or maybe you can help me. I'm qualifying Susan Fairbanks for an apartment rental—"

"Who?"

Natalie repeated the name.

"Um, no. I've never heard of her and I do all the scheduling for my manager," she informed. "If she worked here, I would know. But I've only been here three months, so if she was here before that—"

"Thanks for your time," Natalie said. She was all business and good at creating a cover story. Necessity. He couldn't imagine not being able to put down roots or drive up to the barn and be able to speak to someone he had history with. Her life explained the loneliness he'd seen in her eyes when she thought no one was looking.

"THERE YOU GO." Natalie was happy to contribute, even a little bit. She hoped this would give Jack a few answers or at least point him in a direction. Or maybe she was easing her guilt for preparing to walk out the door.

All the vibrato she'd worked up on the ride over had dissipated like late November snow on a Texas morning. Her plan had been simple. Grab the backpack and ask for a ride to the nearest internet café before she lost her nerve. Preferably north. The pull toward Jack was too strong and she didn't want to break it. The same old logic wound through her thoughts that had her draw the conclusion she had to go.

At this point, it was a matter of willpower. She tried to convince herself this was nothing more than forcing herself out of bed to exercise. There would be pain. It wouldn't feel good while she was doing it. Long term, though, it was best for her. And once she got over the pain, she could rebuild.

The terrible thought she'd never find anyone who fit her as well as Jack struck like lightning from a clear blue sky. The daunting reality that she'd be running away to be alone again for months on end with no one to talk to or share her secrets with was another blow.

The will to live would kick in at some point, erasing all her doubts about whether or not she was making the right decision. Natalie almost laughed out loud. What decision? This was survival at its most basic level. And even if she did call her old handler to ask for a new identity and a new city, she still had to start over. This way, she could keep her new name. Coming up with excuses as to why she didn't have old friends or social media accounts got old. It seemed like everyone was online these days. *Jack wasn't*, a little voice in the back of her head reminded. But then, he was different than most.

Yeah? Jack was amazing. She wouldn't argue there. He was also deeply rooted in Cattle Cove, had a loving family who noticed if he didn't show up somewhere, and worked in a job that he loved. How great would that be?

Speaking of Jack, she looked up in time to catch him studying her.

"What?" she asked, embarrassed that he'd caught her so deep in thought about him.

"You're beautiful. That's all."

Well, why did he have to be so perfect? She could feel the red blush crawl up her neck and flame her cheeks.

"You've helped me out. Now, it's my turn. How can I help you, Natalie? What do you need me to do?" He put his hands up, palms out. "For the record, I don't want you to go.

But you've glanced at the back door half a dozen times since we got back and I don't want to hold you back from something you feel compelled to do."

"That means a lot, Jack. For the same record, I wish I could stay a little longer." She half expected him to capitalize on the admission. Or maybe she just wished he had some magic words that could make everything okay. The truth was that she wasn't okay. And would maybe never be okay again.

His lips compressed.

"I was thinking about how Bernie might need someone here during the day while you're at work and I wish that person could be me." Well, the floodgates were opening now. And while she was at it, she might as well admit she'd been looking at the door thinking how much she didn't want to walk out of it.

"You don't have to tell me your whole plan," Jack started. "Just the next step, so I can help with that. I'd like to make sure you have a safe next step, Natalie. I don't like the feeling of sending you out there alone."

His last word was more of that lightning striking.

"I have a couple of thoughts, if you want to hear them," he said.

She nodded.

"We know a lot of ranchers throughout the country. I could pull in a favor and get you set up at a place in Montana. You'd have shelter and food. The couple who owns the ranch are longtime friends of my family. It's secluded and away from Louisiana."

She was listening.

"Or you could stay here another day or two while we come up with a plan. I have to take care of...*this*." He motioned toward the box on the counter. "I need to make sure no one is in danger. Once this is over, I'd like to know where I can find you again."

Both of those ideas would make her heart sing if they didn't put him in danger. Having information about her could get him killed. Harboring her could get him killed. Covering her tracks could get him killed.

Could she be that selfish? Could she risk his life to save her heart?

"Believe me when I say that I like the sound of either one of those options, Jack. You have no idea how happy either one of them would make me. There's risk—"

"Maybe we could stop right there."

"I trust you to keep the information I told you to yourself. That's a huge step. Now, I have to ask you to trust that I know what I'm doing." She didn't. Not really. She was absolutely certain that she needed to protect Jack, though, and that was the only thing that mattered at this point. "Promise me that you'll respect whatever decision I make about my future."

His expression morphed to disappointment. "I already gave you my word."

And he had a Cowboy Code that said he would back it up. She wasn't asking for him. She was asking for herself. She needed to hear the words come out of his mouth.

"And I'd give it to you again if that's all it takes to make those stress lines on your forehead ease up."

"Thank you." He had no idea how much it meant to her. Then again, looking at him as he closed the distance between them now...maybe he did.

12

"Can you give me one more day?" Jack could do a lot to help Natalie if he had a little more time with her. Convincing her to stick around Cattle Cove wasn't part of the plan, no matter how much he wished it was an option. This was her life. She had to decide what was best, no matter how hard he was falling for her again or how much protection he believed he could offer.

She stood there and he could almost see her mind clicking through her options.

"I'm not asking you to stick around beyond that." To her point, he couldn't watch over her twenty-four-seven, three-hundred-sixty-five days a year. He could reasonably assure her safety while on the ranch. Leave the property and he could offer no such guarantee.

Her social media ban wasn't a problem. He preferred to be as far away from the internet as he could. Long days filled with hard work on the ranch were up his alley, not sitting at a computer or being glued to his phone screen. And although ranching involved far more paperwork than anyone of his family members, including himself, cared to do, most of his time was spent outdoors. Every sunny day, he paused long enough to watch the sun rise in the eastern horizon. It was a sight to behold. The bold orange and bright yellow colors painted an almost endless sky.

Natalie wrung her hands together.

"I'm not trying to make this hard on you. Believe it or not, I want to help in any way I can. If it's better for you to walk out the door and not look back, then by all means." He wouldn't talk about the hit his heart would take. "On the other hand, if lying low for the rest of today while you come up with a plan that doesn't have you running off half-cocked or hitchhiking sounds better, we can do that too."

She tapped her toes on the tile floor.

Knowing when to keep talking and when to keep quiet was a lost art. In this moment, Jack knew without a doubt keeping quiet was the play. So he waited.

After what felt like an eternity but was probably about two minutes, Natalie said, "I'd like to stay."

He waited for the one word he hated in a conversation like this...the inevitable *but*.

"I ran out of Austin so fast that I didn't think it all through. Like, where I was going or what I was going to do when I got there. Once my car died, I had no idea how I was going to move forward." She shook her head. "I was comfortable in Austin and that led to being complacent. I let my guard down, which is easy to do in a city like Austin."

Austin's vibe was definitely laid back even if its traffic was the opposite.

"Being here the past twenty hours or so still hasn't given me a chance to think ahead. I was just trying to catch my breath. You know?"

"I do." He couldn't understand her exact situation, but

he understood being so tired thinking straight became a problem.

"So, yes, staying another day would give me a chance to do just that...think ahead instead of just covering my tracks."

"It would."

She set the backpack down and few of its contents spilled out. She dropped to her knees and scooped up the cash. A twinkle of gold caught his eye.

"Who does the ring belong to?" Curiosity got the best of him. He hoped he wasn't crossing a line.

"My grandmother." Her expression morphed to admiration. She located the band and pulled it out. "This was hers and it's all I have left of her. I wasn't kidding when I told you about wearing it so men wouldn't bother me while I was studying or sitting at the coffee shop. The other part I didn't mention was that it makes me feel close to her whenever I feel lost."

Jack closed the distance between them and helped her replace the contents of the backpack. He picked it up and positioned it on the back of a chair. "What was she like?"

"Strong. And she had a sense of humor like you wouldn't believe. She came from a different generation, you know. And her life was far from easy. She would be talking, and I'd be taking everything so seriously. Then she'd whip out a line that had us both laughing until we cried," she said.

He couldn't help but break out in a smile. Miss Penny could be described in similar ways, and he bet the two of them would have been great friends.

"What happened to her, if you don't mind my asking," he said.

"She passed away three and a half years ago. It's part of the reason I thought I'd be okay going in the program. She was gone and I had no one. My folks were never in the picture. It seemed easy to walk away from my life. Honestly, I think I was too sad to make a sound decision. Then, I witnessed the crime. It was all so accidental me being outside when the murder occurred." The admission, the honesty, struck him in a deep place and chipped away at more of the protective coating around his heart.

"Sounds like bad timing," he said, wishing he could ease some of her pain.

"Yes. I'm pretty famous for it." Her smile was melancholy. "I mean, who goes off half-cocked in her car only to have it break down in the first hour? Seriously? Who does that happen to?"

"I can't account for all the timing, but you won't hear me complain about finding you on the road when I did, Natalie." His voice was a little deeper, a little huskier than normal. He cleared his throat to ease the sudden dryness with the admission.

She practically beamed at him and that did very little to help with the knot forming in his chest.

Needing the change the subject, he said, "I can set you up with a laptop. Teach you how to clear the cache files so no one will be able to see which websites you visited." A true tech person could find anything on a device despite wiping the hard drive clean, but few and far between possessed the knowledge or the skillset to pull it off. So he felt reasonably confident in making the promise.

"Okay. That would be a good place to start. I have my phone too."

Jack disappeared into his office that was located off the kitchen and returned with laptop in hand. He set it down on the table and then booted it up. A minute later, it had worked its magic and was good to go. "What else do you need?"

"A pen and paper would be nice," she said.

He retrieved those items.

"Thank you," she said as he set them down on the table.

"What else? Coffee?" He glanced at the clock on the wall that read half past ten o'clock in the morning. He smiled, remembering his conversation with William. "Lunch?"

Well, now she really smiled at him. "Isn't it a bit early for lunch?"

Aside from the fact they hadn't digested the breakfast tacos yet, probably not. He normally ate in the next half hour or so, depending on how the day was going. Then again, his lunch usually consisted of a sandwich of some kind, a piece of fruit and a bottle of water. Fancy, it was not. The view could be spectacular on a good day, though.

"What will you do?" she asked, already onto her first search on the internet.

"I want to do a little more digging into Susan's situation. See if I can find out where she works and verify that she has a child. It shouldn't be too difficult since I know her address." With the internet, privacy had gone out the window. In this case, he wouldn't complain.

WITHIN TWO HOURS, Natalie had a room booked at a cash-only motel on the outskirts of Tulsa and found two vehicles she could afford to buy that were within twenty miles of her current location. Buying a car would create a serious dent in her cash reserve but she would still have enough to get her somewhere in the northwest where she could get a waitressing job to make up some of the deficit. She'd slept in her vehicle before to get through a rough patch. Was it ideal? Nope. But she'd learned to be resourceful, using truck stops or gyms to shower.

The vehicles' owners should return her texts shortly. Instead of feeling satisfied for a job well done, her heart hurt. Glancing around at all the luxuries, she gave herself a minute to mourn them. There'd be no dishwasher or premade meals where she was going. Oh, wow, she hadn't even thought about how much she was going to miss Miss Penny's cooking. Strange, because she'd only been there a day and Natalie had yet to meet the woman whose skills were right up there with any of the fanciest restaurants in Austin.

She glanced at Jack, who was intensely studying the screen on his smartphone, and her heart took another hit. Ignoring that, she asked, "Do you want me to heat up lunch?"

He immediately pushed to standing.

"No. No. Sit down. It's my turn to spoil you. Goodness knows you've been treating me like royalty ever since I arrived." She waved at him.

He smiled a devastating smile that only made him more handsome. He raked his fingers through his hair. "Guess I've been staring at a device a little too long. It's making me jumpy."

"Same. My eyes will permanently cross if I stare at a screen much longer and my stomach is telling me I should've taken you up on the offer of food earlier this morning," she admitted.

"I can fix drinks, at least," he said. "What sounds good? Lemonade? Tea? Miss Penny keeps this place stocked."

"Tea sounds good. Do I even need to ask if it's already sweetened?"

He feigned disappointment and it was the cutest darn thing she'd seen all day.

"Okay, okay. I take back the question. Sweet tea it is."

"This is Texas, and last I checked we were still considered part of the South." Jack pulled two glasses from the cabinet and filled them with ice cubes and then the drink.

"Technically, we're in the Southwest," she corrected as he moved past her. He looped a hand around her waist as he passed by, pausing long enough to brush his lips against hers.

"Southwest," he repeated.

"But not so southwest that we're in New Mexico. You know?" She took out a container and peeked inside. "Meatloaf? Are you kidding me right now?"

"Looks like it and, no, I would not kid you about food." He laughed, and it literally made her heart sing.

For just this moment in time, for today, she wanted to forget about the fact she was leaving him and everything she'd built for the past three years behind. She wanted to forget that she'd ever met, or in her case *seen*, anyone with the last name Fontenot. She wanted to get lost in this moment because, like a shooting star, it would disappear too soon, never to be experienced again.

She needed to create a memory so strong, so vivid that it would get her through the lonely times that were on the horizon. She needed to wrap herself in the blanket that was Jack, her temporary shelter from a raging storm. The clouds were forming; she could feel them in her bones in the way a person felt rain coming. There would be meals eaten in front of a TV set in a crappy motel. There would be tears—tears that were rare, but they would come. She would cry herself to sleep, wishing she could get off this merry-go-round that had become her life.

Feeling sorry for herself? Check.

That would come. Not now. Now, she needed to be with Jack without the nagging thought her life was about to change again.

It was a strange sensation to be back on the run again. To *need* to be back on the run, she corrected. Once she left this house, that was it. All the progress she'd made in Austin would be gone. The slate wiped clean.

The notion had once comforted her. Now, it felt like a prison sentence.

Being anywhere Jack wasn't felt like a prison sentence, she corrected. And since that line of thinking was super unproductive and fell into the category of Not Helping, she pushed it aside. Today was for her and Jack.

If this experience could teach her one thing, it was to live in the moment. Easy to say, hard to do.

The microwave beeped, cutting into her thoughts. Jack was in her peripheral, clearing room on the table and breaking out the napkins. The two of them worked like a well-rehearsed dance. She dished out the portions onto plates and then brought them to the table, as well.

He stood back and examined the table. "Something isn't quite right." He had a twinkle in his eye as he held up a finger. "Hold on a sec."

He disappeared outside for a few seconds and then came back inside holding a couple of wildflowers. He grabbed a glass, filled it with water and then proudly set the makeshift vase on the table. "If I'm only going to get a couple more meals with you, I want them to be perfect."

Well, didn't those words melt more of the protective barrier she'd placed around her heart. It would be so easy to let her guard down again with him. She'd done it once already. Jack McGannon had a way of slipping past the gate when it came to her. Logic flew out the window anytime she was near him.

When she really thought about it, that had been part of the reason for the breakup. She'd panicked when she realized how quickly and easily he affected her. There'd never been anyone in her life who made her feel the way Jack did. He had a way of listening to her, of hearing her, of encouraging her that was unmatched in past relationships.

But then Jack McGannon was an easy person to fall for.

None of that mattered right now. She let herself get carried away in what turned into the most romantic lunch of her life. She tried to convince herself this was a last hurrah and that was the reason it felt so special. But that was Jack. He made everything better.

And since that thinking would only lead her further down the trail of needing him, she changed the subject. "I got so busy with my work, I forgot to ask if there'd been any word on Bernie. How's he doing?"

"Good." Jack took a bite of food.

"Everything is going okay, I take it?"

"All is well. He's going to be fine. He still has to get through surgery, though."

For reasons she couldn't explain and didn't want to examine, she burst out into tears.

13

"I'm sorry."

"There you go apologizing again. I didn't realize my conversation skills were that bad," Jack teased. His joke worked because she burst out laughing.

"I'm not normally a leaky faucet," she explained as he thumbed away a tear.

"You don't have to do that with me," he reassured. "You don't have to explain yourself. Besides, you're one of the strongest people I've ever known. Don't feel bad for crying. Most people wouldn't survive a day in your shoes. If a few tears help relieve some of your stress, it's not a big deal."

His reassurance was met with the warmest smile—a smile that could defrost the freezer with the door shut.

"Why do you have to be so damn understanding?" she teased. And he was pretty sure he also heard, "And so damn perfect."

"Well, I can assure you that I'm not perfect. So, no worries there." He stood up and cleared the empty plates. "Miss Penny's meatloaf is another story altogether. That might actually be perfect."

He was rewarded with another smile just as his phone buzzed. Another text. He walked over to it and checked the screen.

You can't keep ignoring me, Jack. Our daughter deserves a better father. We all pay for our sins. If you won't help me, she'll pay.

If those words weren't scary, he didn't know what would be.

"Is it from her?" Natalie asked.

"Yes."

Natalie repositioned so she could read the text. She blew out a breath. "This is serious. You don't think she'd hurt the little girl to get back at you, do you?"

"No arguments there and I have no idea what she's capable of." What did that last part mean? His daughter would pay? Jack didn't like the sound of that.

"She seems even more agitated. Maybe the dispatcher was wrong about not responding to her. By ignoring her, it's like adding gas to a burning fire."

"I had the same thought just now." There was no way he could sit idle when a threat like that had been issued.

His phone buzzed again. Natalie stared at it like it was a bomb about to detonate.

first you kick me out of your bed.

...

then you kick me out of your life.

...

now you call the cops on me.

...

He waited for the last text to come through after seeing three dots on the screen that indicated she was typing. Nothing. He checked the number of bars to see if connectivity was a problem. Nope.

"Maybe she thought better of what she was about to say," Natalie said by way of explanation.

"That might be optimistic." The fact she could fathom the positive in a negative situation was one of her many amazing traits.

"This just feels like a cry for help in a dark, twisted way," she reasoned.

"The Susan I knew wasn't this..." He let her comment sit. "I can't help but think something might have happened to her."

"Like a trauma?"

"Something like that. A car crash or injury," he said. "My mind snaps to my dad's situation. For a long time, the doctors weren't sure what he would be like when he woke from the coma."

"Traumatic brain injury," she said. "I had a neighbor who worked as a nurse in a trauma ward. We talked a few times when we saw each other at our mailboxes. She would tell me stories that would blow your hair back. People definitely change after suffering trauma."

"I can't help but think we dodged a bullet with Dad. He knows who he is and his mind is as sharp as ever. His body is recovering. With his age, it's taking a little more time to get there but that's to be expected."

"It's amazing that he woke up rearing to go with all his mental faculties," she agreed.

"He has no memory of the accident."

"None at all?" She reached across the table and touched his hand. The motion happened so smoothly, he doubted she'd even thought about it.

He shook his head. "It's the reason we can't clear Uncle Donny. Without Dad's memory of the events, we only have my uncle's to go on, and he's currently the chief suspect."

"Why would he hurt your father? What would he have to gain by it?"

"Apparently, he'd been consulting a lawyer about challenging Dad's sole ownership of the ranch."

She balked. "After cashing out his inheritance and then gambling all the money away?"

"Guess he feels entitled to more."

"What a jerk." She flashed eyes at him. "Sorry. I know he's your family and everything, but he sounds like a real piece of work."

"Everyone has an Uncle Donny in the family," he conceded.

"I think both my parents fit into that category." She squeezed his fingers. "Your dad welcomed him home and gave him a role around the ranch."

"He wants more. The sheriff isn't talking about what other evidence she has after arresting him. Uncle Donny has been stirring up trouble in the family. For example, reaching out to our long-lost brother. Don't get me wrong, part of me is glad he did. Now, we know about Kurt. But my gut feeling is that Uncle Donny contacted our brother to bring him here and stir up trouble. He obviously broke our dad's trust." Jack didn't mention the part about being disappointed in his father—a man Jack and the others had always put on a pedestal. Clive McGannon was the epitome of hard work building success. Jack and his brothers had believed their parents' marriage had been a strong one. Clive never remarried after losing his wife. He dated around a little but never seemed able to replace their mother. Or, at least not in his mind.

"People deflect attention when they want to shift the focus from themselves," she said.

"Exactly. If he, say, pushed my father off a tractor instead of Dad falling, that wouldn't be just wrong and immoral. That would be attempted murder."

"How awful would that be for your family?"

"My cousins have been taking it hard, as anyone might expect. They might not have grown up close to their father but they, like the rest of us, don't want to think he's capable of such atrocity."

"Understandable."

He nodded.

"Speaking of crimes, I need to decide what to do." He motioned toward his cell phone at almost the exact instant another text came through.

i'm sorry.

...

i didn't mean it

...

forgive me?

...

we can make this right

...

give me another chance?

"The tone of these texts has certainly changed." So much so, he was trying to avoid whiplash.

"Are you going to answer?"

"I think I have to." He typed in a message.

where are you?

The response came fast.

guess

He typed in his response.

cattle cove?

There were a few beats of silence.

austin

He looked up at Natalie. "What do you think? Can we trust her to tell the truth at this point?"

"Good question. I hope so."

He typed another message:

are you okay?

No response came.

Jack got up and made a cup of coffee, figuring the old saying about a watched pot never boiling might be true in this case. He looked to Natalie and held up his cup. "Want one?"

"No, thanks." She stared at the phone too.

Jack might not have gotten a response from Susan, but he got a hit from one of his inquiries about her. His cell indicated an e-mail came through. Good. He was about to find out something else about her. He moved to the table, fresh coffee in hand. He set it down before picking up his phone.

Natalie had gone back to working on her notes. She ripped off the top page, folded it and placed it inside her backpack, a reminder that sharing information wasn't a two-way street.

A couple of swipes later, and his e-mail was pulled up. There were dozens, reminding him that he was neglecting his work at the ranch. But the one on top caught his eye. The subject line read: Employment.

Jack ran his thumb over the message, pulling it up on the screen. He bit back a curse.

"Which coffee shop did you say you were at when you believed that someone poisoned you?" An ominous feeling settled over him.

"The one I always go to on Congress Avenue. Austin Grinds. I took you there..." It seemed to dawn on her.

"Do you remember who took your order? Was the person male or female?"

"Female. A beautiful brunette, actually."

"Susan," he said under his breath.

"Do you have a picture of her?" Natalie's mind seemed to be clicking through possibilities after this new information.

He nodded, and then found one on his phone.

"That's her." Natalie crossed her arms over her chest in a defensive move.

He didn't want to go there. He didn't want to believe the possibility that Susan had somehow put two-and-two together. "How could she have put the two of us together?"

"This." Natalie picked up her phone and showed him the screen saver. It was a close-up picture of the two of them, looking deliriously happy. "She asked about that picture when she brought my order to the table. I didn't think much about her reaction to it at the time."

"And you were wearing a gold band." It was possible Susan's mind snapped but there had to be more to it than realizing Jack was together with someone else. Plus, she hadn't brought up anything about a marriage. Though, he had been ignoring her. That alone might have angered her if she was unstable.

"Yep. I'm also really regretting the decision not to call Austin P.D. or, at the very least, take the substance in to the lab on my own. The intention could have been to make me sick, not kill me. My mind just immediately went to the threat I already knew."

"We have no idea what her intention was," he agreed.

"Nope. Without analysis, we don't know if she was trying to hurt me or kill me. Maybe she was trying to make me sick or warn me off of you."

He picked up his phone as anger and frustration burned

through him. Had she crossed a dangerous line in trying to hurt Natalie? His grip tightened around the cell. So hard, in fact, his knuckles went white. Susan had no right to target Natalie. Was she trying to hurt her or kill her? The latter was almost unimaginable. Using poison to scare someone was almost just as bad. Then, there was the paternity accusation.

Even if Susan was trying to get rid of someone she would view as competition, it still didn't explain the timing of why she would wait until her baby was five months old to tell him. Why bring the baby news up now? What was he missing?

He tried to ease his grip on the cell as he brought up the web search engine. He typed in the words, Austin Grinds. The name came up along with location and phone number. He touched the number on the screen and the phone automatically connected the call. He put the cell on speaker and took another sip of his own coffee.

"Austin Grinds, how can I help you?" A perky male voice answered.

"I'm trying to reach someone who works there. Her name is Susan Fairbanks."

"You're a little late for that. She never showed for work yesterday. Apparently, she sent a text to our manager that she wasn't coming back," the worker said. "Of all the nerve, she tried to get him to pay her. Not only will she not get any money out of this place, but she just killed her chance of ever getting a reference, too."

"Thank you for your time." Jack ended the call and looked up at Natalie. Both seemed to realize what must have happened. "I'm sorry, Nat—"

"Not your fault, Jack."

That didn't stop him from feeling somehow responsible.

Maybe he should have answered Susan's texts. Would that have made a difference? Would that have stopped her? Would that have spared Natalie?

The only positive thing about this whole ordeal was getting to see Natalie again. Logic might argue otherwise, but it was good for his heart.

At least for now.

14

"If she's responsible for trying to hurt you..."

"We don't know that yet." On so many levels, Natalie wanted it to be true. She wanted Susan to be responsible for the coffee shop threat because it would mean her identity hadn't been discovered. That, maybe she could reclaim her life in Austin, a life that she loved. As much as she wanted it to, nothing would change between her and Jack. Her heart ached at the thought. He was still high profile and she most definitely couldn't afford her face to show up on social media or some society page, but that didn't stop her heart from beating faster every time he came close. And the feel of his lips weren't less imprinted on hers because a relationship wasn't in the cards.

If she could go there with anyone, it would be him. Life had taught her that wishes were for little kids holding coins in front of a water fountain. In the grown-up world, the fairy tale didn't exist.

Needing to do something besides sit there, she got up and made another cup of coffee. "Want a refill?"

He nodded as he studied his screen.

"I hope your association with me didn't put you in any danger." He frowned as she set the cup down in front of him.

"It wouldn't be your fault and, believe it or not, I'd rather it be a known entity. And not someone who has a stronghold in organized crime," she admitted. "A normal person can be stopped. The family who would be after me has long arms."

"A known enemy?"

"Something like that," she said.

"You shouldn't be in a position to have an enemy at all."

"I spent a lot of time in regret, wishing my life could've somehow turned out differently. What if it had? I never would've met you. So, I can't regret any of it. I might switch a few things around." She laughed at the last line, hoping it would break some of the tension. They'd been on pins and needles since finding out about Susan.

Jack leaned in and kissed her so gently it robbed her of her breath. Her heart beat wildly in her chest, hammering her ribs. And her stomach freefell like she was base jumping.

So, no, she didn't regret the time they'd spent together. Not even when the breakup hurt so badly that she didn't want to get out of bed for a solid week.

She'd forced herself to, though. And when it was too much to think about getting through a whole day, she broke it down to making it through an hour. The times when getting through an hour was too much, she focused on getting through the next minute. Until eventually she could not only think about a day, but a whole week at a time.

Life was like that. When it got hard, she had to shrink time...move step by step...until she could regain her footing and think longer term.

When he pulled back, he pressed his forehead against hers. "I missed you, Natalie. Is it okay to admit that?"

It was more than okay, her heart practically danced.

"I missed you too, Jack." More than she would ever let on to herself. She'd gotten a little too good at suppressing her feelings and marching ahead. Shoving her feelings down deep where they stayed buried. And in the process, she could admit that she'd stopped living. Being in fear all the time took a toll. Granted, the threat was still there. She couldn't let her guard down or allow pictures of her to surface. But she could breathe a sigh of relief now. All signs pointed to Susan being responsible for the café incident.

Had Natalie overreacted by getting out of there, packing up and taking off?

For Susan...yes.

If it had been Fontenot...no.

Jack's phone pinged again, indicating another e-mail. He pulled it up and read, "*Susan Fairchild gave birth to a six-and-a-half-pound baby girl.*" He glanced up at Natalie. "The dates match up to Susan's claim of having a child roughly five months ago." He refocused on the phone in his hand and his face morphed to one of sadness and compassion. "The little girl died two weeks ago from SIDS."

"Sudden Infant Death Syndrome," Natalie said quietly. She'd heard of it but couldn't imagine the amount of pain that would come with losing a child. And that loss could trigger a breakdown.

"There was no wrongdoing on the part of the mother, according to the article that came up in my search."

"Oh. Jack. That's so sad. How awful and how tragic for a mother to have to go through something like that." Don't get her wrong, the thought Susan would come after Natalie was more than unsettling. It was criminal and she needed to be stopped before she succeeded. No question there.

"It's unimaginable to lose a child, especially one so young," he agreed and there was so much sadness in those words.

"It could explain Susan's erratic behavior." She put her hands up, palms out. "I'm not defending her, and I absolutely believe she's going about this all the wrong way. But it does give us insight into why she might be having some sort of mental breakdown at this point."

He nodded, stared at the phone.

The thought this could be his child too crossed her mind. Wouldn't Susan have contacted him before now? Having McGannon attached to her child's last name would be a benefit to the kid as well as the mother. *If it was true.*

She knew better than to ask him outright. If he was the father, he would need a minute to process. And maybe he never would be ready to talk about it with her. The child was gone.

Natalie's heart ached for Jack and the possibility that he'd lost a child and he'd only just found out this was a possibility. She couldn't begin to imagine what it must be like to carry a child for nine months, give birth and then lose the sweet angel before her first birthday. There couldn't be much worse in this world than losing a child. Looking back, her server had seemed exhausted. Hadn't she mentioned something about being up all night with her baby? Obviously a lie because her baby would have been gone by then. Such a terrible turn of events. Such sad news. Such a terrible fate.

Losing a child could cause someone to lose touch with reality.

Jack looked up at her. He had been studying his phone

intently. "According to the birth certificate, the kid's last name was Holland. Susan's is Fairbanks."

"Did she list the father's name?"

"Doesn't seem so."

Didn't necessarily mean the child wasn't Jack's. But it did raise questions.

JACK'S HEART ached for Susan. Losing a child could explain her erratic behavior. She'd been through more than any person should have to go through. But questions remained. Was she dangerous? How far would she go? Could she be stopped?

"What do you think about hanging out at the ranch for a few days until this situation is resolved?" Jack didn't like the thought of Natalie being out there, away from him, where he couldn't personally protect her. And he'd made up his mind about involving law enforcement. Sheriff Justice needed to know about the 'gift' and be informed of the possibility of Susan returning to town.

Natalie bit her bottom lip. "Seems like a good idea."

Her hesitation, what she didn't say, was that it would also make it harder to leave. Yeah, he felt that in the burn inside his chest. But until Susan was safely out of the picture, he would worry.

Some of his ideas from earlier came to mind. Like, revisiting the idea of Natalie moving to Montana to work on a ranch there.

He'd bring that up again once the Susan threat was cleared. As much as his heart was breaking for her right now, he wouldn't underestimate her. She'd crossed a line there might not be a way back from.

"I need to give the sheriff a call to update her," he said to Natalie. "Make yourself at home."

"Okay." She smiled up at him and there was so much compassion in her eyes. He bent down and pressed a kiss to her lips before walking outside.

He needed to reconnect with the land he loved. Being cooped up indoors was getting to him. He needed fresh air in order to think more clearly.

He could admit to a certain amount of relief in finding out the kid had a different last name than his or Susan's, no doubt named after her father. In Jack's heart of hearts, he didn't believe the baby was his. And yet, a piece of him felt connected to the little girl, the sadness that came with knowing what had happened.

This was also the first time he'd considered whether he ever wanted to be a father at some point. With the right person, he was beginning to warm up to the idea of starting a family.

Jack took a minute to walk off the mix of emotion coursing through him; sadness for the loss, anger for the fact Susan targeted Natalie, frustration that he couldn't help or make it stop.

The call to Sheriff Justice took ten minutes. She promised to reach out to Austin P.D. to give them an update. It took another couple of minutes to forward the e-mails he'd received and the screenshots he'd taken.

Being outside grounded him, gave him the space to think clearly. His thoughts drifted to Bernie and all the ways in which he'd need to get ready for the big fella. His next call was to Derek's personal line. The vet didn't pick up right away.

After a walk to his favorite spot near the creek, Jack took

in a few deep breaths to clear the cobwebs. His cell buzzed in his hand and Derek's name filled the screen.

"I just finished up with pre-op for Bernie." There was a quality to Derek's voice that sent up alarm bells.

"Is everything going okay?"

"For the most part, yes. Surgery is never easy, and he's been through a lot leading up to it. I wouldn't operate if I didn't think he was ready."

"Can I come see him?"

"I wouldn't advise it right now. Give him a few hours to recover. I'll give you a call as soon as he's in the clear."

Jack didn't like the sound of that, but he respected Derek's judgment. The day had gone by in a blur and he figured it wouldn't hurt to get some rest now that Natalie agreed to stay on a few days.

"He'll be okay, though. Right?"

"His vitals are improving. He's moving in the right direction." Derek paused. "I know that's not exactly what you want to hear, but I'm personally watching over him. He'll get my full attention."

"Thank you. It means a lot to hear." Jack thanked the family friend before ending the call and heading back inside. He and Natalie must've had the same idea because she was already showered and resting when he walked into the bedroom. He followed suit, joining her after laying out his clothes next to the bed so he'd be ready when the call came in.

When Natalie rolled over and curled her body around his, he thought he could stay in this position forever.

Before he knew it, they were both asleep.

It only seemed like a few minutes passed when the phone buzzed. Jack reached around on the nightstand, fumbling for his cell. He knocked it off, cursed and tried to shake off the fog with very little success.

He rolled over and located the phone on the carpet, still buzzing.

"Hello," he said, sitting up ramrod straight after reading the name on the screen.

"Bernie is doing better now," Derek began. "He started vomiting and we had to get his blood pressure under control."

"How is he now?" Jack could feel his own blood pressure shoot through the roof.

"Stabilized. His vitals are strong. I wanted you to be the first to know what's going on," Derek said.

"I'll be right there." Jack ended the call and looked over at Natalie, who was surprisingly still asleep through the call. Seeing her long wavy hair splayed across the pillow made the world seem right again.

Rather than wake her, he decided to leave a note in case she woke before he returned. She looked so peaceful and he wished he could give her a thousand nights of peaceful sleep.

Coincidence or maybe just dumb luck had brought her home. He just wished he could find a way for her to stay.

15

Natalie woke to the sound of glass breaking down the hall. At first, she thought she'd dreamt the noise. Hearing it a second time confirmed her fear. Someone was breaking in.

Her pulse skyrocketed. She reached around for her clothes. Couldn't find them.

Since Jack had a key and the mystery guest didn't, Natalie had no plans to stick around. Fear caused her chest to squeeze. She breathed through it as she reached around for anything she could use as a weapon.

There wasn't much to work with other than a lamp. It could do some damage if she struck at the right angle. Better yet, could she get out of there and avoid a confrontation altogether?

Best case scenario? She could climb out a window and slip into the woods. Tentacles of fear wrapped around her, squeezing her.

She glanced at the clock and saw a note. She picked it up and rubbed her eyes. Jack was with Bernie after he experienced complications with surgery. She reached for her phone and realized it was still in her backpack in the other room. Knowing Jack, he would have already texted an update by now. She must have been dead asleep for him to leave her in bed. And she hoped it was also a sign Bernie's situation wasn't dire.

A creek in the wood flooring in the hallway caused her to jump. Jack?

Her instincts kicked in and she moved to the door, back against the wall. She listened. There were no lights on down the hallway and there should be more noise. The hairs on the back of her neck prickled.

Something was off and she had no plans to stick around to find out only to be too late to save herself. She moved to the nearest window, unlocked it and forced it open. She knocked the screen loose and kicked it out of the way, climbing onto the ledge. Thank heaven for first floor master bedrooms.

Not waiting around to see if anyone followed, she looked both ways and then sprinted across the yard. The hard Texas dirt let her know instantly that she didn't have on shoes. And lights came on at the side of the house, casting a spotlight on her.

She could only pray the intruder was in the hallway and couldn't see the bright lights.

Panting for air, she crouched low in the scrub brush directly behind the house. Pure instinct told her to stay put. A shadow passed by the second window in the bedroom. A female. There was only one person who would sneak into Jack's house in the middle of the night...Susan.

Jack would be back soon, and Natalie needed a way to warn him. Her phone was still tucked inside her backpack inside the house. Where was it? *Kitchen*. The word came to her instantly.

No. No. No. This couldn't be happening. It was pitch-black outside, and the creepy-sounding cicadas chirped in the background, causing her skin to prickle and the hairs on the back of her neck to stand on end.

Mosquitos were having a field day with her and this wasn't the time to remember she had on boxers and a T-shirt with her bare feet. She had to move along the brush and circle around the house to the front where Jack's Jeep would come in.

For a few seconds, she debated leaving the perimeter altogether and heading toward the main house or the security shack. Right now, she knew Susan was inside the house. This was the best place to keep an eye on the woman no matter how many bug bites Natalie had to suffer.

She also needed to be able to signal Jack. He would have his phone and could call 911. The plan seemed easy enough as long as Susan stayed put inside the house.

Natalie kept one eye on the house as she moved through the tree line. If she stepped onto the grassy area of the yard, those automatic lights would give away her location. She had no idea what kind of weapon Susan might be carrying and didn't want to risk finding out.

Winding her way around toward the front of the house, branches slapped her face and her feet were shredded.

Out of the corner of her eye, she saw someone slip out the bedroom window. Natalie dropped down onto all fours and then froze. She made herself as small as possible, blocking out all the potential creepy-crawlers around her. She could only pray there were no spiders. A cat walked over her grave thinking about them. Beady eyes. Eight legs. Spider webs.

This was not the time to freak herself out. A shadow moved around the house. It was too far away to see clearly at this distance even with the lights on. She couldn't make out details, but the overall shape was female.

The woman had lost her baby and that had caused her to snap. She'd fixated on Jack. Those were facts. She apparently also convinced herself that Natalie was the reason Jack had left. All scary thoughts, especially considering she'd somehow made it past ranch security.

Jack had said it would be crazy for Susan to show up in Cattle Cove. Sheriff Justice was on alert as were her deputies. Security at the ranch was also aware and on the lookout. But the property was massive and there were too many blind spots, too many places to slip through if someone was determined. And, Jack hadn't felt a need for extra security around his home, his sanctuary, since poachers never came this close to the residences.

The call that had Jack rushing off to check on Bernie. Natalie's skin crawled at the fact a stranger was keeping such close tabs on their every move, on the details of their lives. She involuntarily shivered and then tried to shake it off. Because the person intent on breaking them up permanently was moving in her direction.

Natalie stilled and tried to slow her breathing. She didn't believe Susan knew she was heading toward Natalie. Not with the way her head kept turning, scanning the woods, searching. Face twisted in desperation, anger and what looked a lot like mania, Susan grunted with frustration.

She had on a white summer dress and some kind of long overcoat, too thick for the moderate temperatures. She was a beacon of contrast. Her disheveled appearance a literal warning not to approach.

Could Natalie slip back inside the house? It was risky

with the motion detector lights. On second thought, it was better to be outside. As Susan moved around to the front of the house, Natalie followed best as she could without drawing attention.

A vehicle's engine hummed. Natalie moved to head it off. Susan disappeared around the opposite side of the house.

Natalie bolted toward the sound of the vehicle. Jack wasn't due back for hours. Did he figure out what Natalie had assumed? The call from the vet's office was bogus.

She was fifteen feet inside the tree line as the Jeep passed by. Natalie pushed to break through as branches slapped her face and torso. She bolted out of the woods and onto the drive waving her arms in the air wildly. She didn't want to risk screaming. Jack might not hear her anyway, but Susan almost certainly would.

Brake lights lit up. The Jeep surged forward to a hard stop. Then came reverse lights as the Jeep spun toward her. She hopped to the side to give Jack room. The tires slid on the gravel as he brought the Jeep to a complete stop.

"She's here. She broke into the house and I climbed out the bedroom window," she said after opening the door and climbing into the passenger seat. She didn't dare risk taking her eyes off the house.

"I didn't see a vehicle," he said.

"And I didn't hear one, either. I literally woke up to the sound of a window breaking down the hallway and then got out of there as fast as I could." Adrenaline had kicked in, temporarily blocking the pain of feet slick from blood.

"Do you know where she is now?" The sound of his voice calmed her nerves a notch below panic. He'd always had that calming effect on her and, like shade on a Texas summer day, it was one of the many draws she felt toward him.

"Lost her when she went around the side of the house." She pointed, keeping her gaze steady ahead.

Jack fished out his cell while he left the engine idling. It rumbled instead of purred like in her sedan. His first call was to security. His second was to the sheriff. He ended the call with a frown.

"What do we do now?" Natalie didn't want Susan to escape.

"This is probably going to sound like a stupid question and one I should have asked sooner, but did you get a good look at her?" Jack asked.

"It's her."

"Then, we wait for reinforcements." The tightness in his tone said he didn't like the idea any more than she did. "We keep watch to make sure she doesn't sneak up from behind us or hit us from the sides."

"We're parked in the woods."

"Yes. Move any closer and she might come out with guns blazing." He reached in the back floorboard and brought a shotgun back. "We don't know what's in her arsenal."

She relayed the description of what she was wearing.

"A white dress? As in *wedding* dress?"

"Could be. Not the traditional tight bodice with a train, but it could work on a destination wedding." Another shiver raced up her spine. "Her hair was a mess, though. And she looked a little bit manic."

He rocked his head.

"I've never been in a situation where I lost a baby before. I'm not sure what that would do to a person," she admitted. She'd heard horror stories about women and postpartum depression. An otherwise balanced person who literally plunged into depression or manic states. "If the baby was only five months old, Susan could be suffering from a medical condition."

"It would explain a lot about her behavior. When we were together, she got clingy a little too fast for my taste but there weren't any signs that she had psychological issues. I count myself as a decent judge of character and with the last name McGannon, I had to figure out early on who could be trusted." He issued a sharp sigh. "She's crossed a criminal line. It's hard to come back from that. But the sheriff's office will have resources to support her."

"I just hope she doesn't do anything that will tie our hands." As Natalie finished her sentence, a hard object landed on the Jeep's roof. A cry sounded, half wild banshee and half dying animal. Another thud practically dented the roof.

"Any chance I can convince you to wait in the Jeep?"

She pressed her lips together and shook her head.

"Didn't figure. Let's go at the same time on my count."

"If you bring that shotgun with you, she'll feel even more threatened. It might back her into a corner," Natalie said.

"She's dangerous. I can't allow her to hurt you," came the quick response.

"I still think it stays inside the Jeep. We can lock the doors."

"It's too risky," he said.

"So is bringing it with us."

The banshee cries turned into howls. Painful-sounding howls.

Jack tucked the shotgun under the seat in the floorboard and then turned the engine off. He tossed over the keys. "I don't know who she'll come after first. If it's me, I'll draw her away from the vehicle. If that's the case, I want you to take off."

She started to argue but he showed his palm, stopping her. She'd won the first battle. She wouldn't win the second. Fair enough.

Besides, she could use the keys as a weapon if she got jumped. She palmed the key fob and then fisted her right hand. There were two other keys, a house key and something that looked like it would open a shed. She positioned those between her fingers with the jagged edges pointing out. A hard jab in the right spot would definitely do some damage.

"On three." He locked gazes and she nodded.

"One. Two. *Three.*"

JACK THREW the door open and hopped out of the Jeep. He heard the doors lock the minute he slammed his shut. "Susan. Over here."

The look in Susan's eyes was a mix of anger and hurt. She had the look of someone who'd been pushed over the edge by grief. The utter desperation and distress in her eyes were a gut punch.

Until they zeroed in on Natalie. And then there was only hate. Susan pounced as she unleashed a shrill scream. Natalie drew back her fist and released a blow as Susan came down on her, knocking them both to the ground.

Jack bolted around the front of the vehicle a few seconds too late. Susan was on her back, Natalie on top of her facing Jack. Susan's legs wrapped around Natalie in a scissor-like grip.

"Stop right there," Jack demanded when he saw the glint of metal.

"Tell him," Susan urged. Her smile one of victory.

"Don't come any closer." The blade was pressed to Natalie's throat in front of her jugular. There was enough pressure to make a dent but no blood.

"You don't want to do this, Susan." Jack held his palms up to show he didn't have a weapon. Natalie had been right. The shotgun would have most likely put Susan over the edge. "You haven't done anything that you can't come back from yet."

"They took my baby, Jack." She sounded pitiful and her face twisted up like she was about to cry. No tears came. Only a haunting laughter that would ring in his ears for the rest of his life. "They took *your* baby."

"The baby wasn't mine, Susan. I think we both know that." He took a stab in the dark with his comment. "You would have told me before now, but that doesn't make me less sorry for your loss." He had no training in how to deal with someone having a psychotic episode. And the sound of vehicles coming nearly sent her over the edge. No doubt, security was arriving.

Jack's phone was inside the Jeep.

Natalie grunted as Susan's grip tightened around her.

"Make whoever that is go away," Susan warned. She didn't argue with his assessment of the situation. "Or I'll slit her throat."

"Okay. Okay. Hold on. I'll do whatever you need me to, just stay calm." He used the same tone with her that he did with the animals when they were agitated. "Let me walk behind the Jeep and up the drive to stop them. Don't do anything until I get back. Okay?"

She leered at him and Natalie clamped her eyes shut.

"I need your word, Susan. I'll come right back. Just hold on for me, okay?"

"Go. I won't do anything yet. I want you to watch when I kill her."

Didn't that cause icy fingers to grip his spine?

Walking away was just about the hardest thing he'd ever done.

16

The knife pressed to Natalie's throat nicked her skin enough to cause a few droplets of blood to roll down her neck. Any slight shift or subtle movement could cause the blade to cut deeper.

Slow breaths, she reminded. *No sudden movement. Clear mind.*

If an opportunity presented itself, she wouldn't hesitate. Right now, all she could do was bide her time. Trying to speak could be dangerous.

"He doesn't love you and he never will. He loves me. He just doesn't realize it yet, but he will. And then he'll drop you so fast your head will spin," the desperate whispers filled Natalie's ear.

It was her compassion that had caused her to hesitate. When she'd slammed her keyed fist into Susan's ribs, she'd howled like she'd been killed. She'd said she was sorry and in that split second of indecision, gained the advantage that could cost Natalie dearly.

She couldn't allow herself to think the mistake would cost her life. Thinking, no *knowing,* that she would walk away from this situation alive and intact was the only tether of hope she could allow.

Jack's urgent footsteps returned, and she opened her eyes in time to see the relief on his face that she was still alive.

"They're gone. I sent them away. Now, let's just you and I talk this through." His voice was a beacon of calm in a raging storm.

Susan started rocking back and forth, her shaky hand moved enough for Natalie to breathe without fear of being sliced. Could she spin out of Susan's grip altogether?

"Do you want to go inside and talk this out?" Jack's question agitated Susan. The rocking intensified. He put his palms toward them. "Slow down there. It's all good if you want to stay out here. I thought you'd be more comfortable inside. We could put on a pot of coffee. I still have the half and half you use."

"You remembered?" The hope in Susan's voice was pitiful.

Natalie would feel worse for the woman if she didn't have a knife rammed against Natalie's skin.

"Of course, I do."

"What we had was special, wasn't it? That's why you remember."

"I wouldn't have spent time with anyone who wasn't special."

"She's not." Natalie could feel Susan's muscles tense.

"We aren't talking about her right now, Susan." He took a step closer. "In fact, she doesn't need to be here. She's a distraction."

Natalie appreciated him taking the tactic of wanting to protect her by getting her out of there, but she wouldn't leave him alone with a woman in a manic state. If Natalie could just get a little distance between her and Susan, get some breathing room.

"She's the problem. She took my baby away." Susan released a wail that would make the most hardened person sad.

"Not her. She doesn't even know you," Jack said. And then came, "It's my fault the baby's gone. I took her."

Susan pushed Natalie off her and then lunged toward Jack with the knife.

Natalie pivoted and grabbed hold of Susan's legs. She went down face first but not before dropping her hand and slicing the back of Natalie's hand. Blood squirted as sirens sounded in the distance.

"No. No. No. No one takes my baby away from me," she chanted and with superhuman-like strength twisted around until she was face-to-face with Natalie.

Fury in her eyes, she brought her hand up high before bringing it down hard to stab Natalie. Except that Susan's hand stopped midway and Jack wrangled the knife away from her before tossing it out of the way.

More of those desperate cries came out of her.

"Get in the Jeep and get to security," Jack said as he basically clamped Susan in a bear hug from behind. He picked her up as he stood, and she pitched a fit.

"I'm not leaving." Natalie located the knife and keys before locking the weapon inside the Jeep. She palmed the keys as Susan tried to kick and fight against Jack's hold. "The sheriff is going to be here any second. We can help you if you let us."

Susan screamed and kicked like she was possessed.

The pain of losing a child must be unimaginable. No one should ever have to go through it. Life could be unfair in taking a little one so young. A child's death was against the natural order, and that's why it had to be excruciating.

"I'm sorry about your daughter, Susan. I really am," Natalie continued, praying she could break through to the woman.

Susan's response was to try to kick Natalie.

"No mother should have to go through what you've been through, Susan. It's unfair." Those were the only words of comfort Natalie could offer. So, she repeated them like a mantra.

"What do you know about me and my pain?" Susan was so worked up she was practically foaming at the mouth. In fact, she spit toward Natalie. She jumped out of the way in time but maintained eye contact, figuring that was her only hope in reaching Susan.

"I don't. I don't have the first clue what you're going through. Most people don't. Most people will never know that kind of suffering and it's so unfair that you are."

Susan slumped onto the ground. Jack made eye contact with Natalie for a split second before refocusing on Susan. She was still a threat and he was smart to keep watch on her. Natalie hoped her words were penetrating, offering some sense of comfort, hollow as that might be, in comparison to what Susan was going through.

There had to be some therapy or medication, or both, that could help her find some kind of balance again. She was obviously a decent person, whose loss of her daughter had broken her beyond relief.

"It's not fair, Susan." Natalie repeated the words a few more times.

Muscles slack, Susan coiled and then sprung at Natalie, snapping her teeth within a foot of Natalie's face. She jerked backward as Jack pulled Susan in the opposite direction.

"What do you know about what I'm going through? You don't know me. You took my baby. My sweet baby girl."

Natalie had never seen someone so vicious and then so pitiful all within the space of a few seconds. She chalked it up to the mania and tried not to take it personally.

The sheriff's SUV roared up, kicking up a dust storm.

Jack coughed but kept his grip tight on Susan as the sheriff parked her vehicle, apologized for the dust, and then zip cuffed Susan. The sheriff looked Natalie up and down.

"Are you injured?"

Natalie brought her hand up to her throat and then examined it. "Nothing a good bandage and antibiotic ointment can't fix."

The sheriff nodded toward Natalie's hand. "You sure about that?"

"Yes." Natalie paused for a second before adding, "She's not in her right mind."

"It's not my call," the sheriff responded. "I'll request a psych evaluation and make certain she has access to every resource in my department."

Natalie nodded.

Jack took in a few deep breaths before turning to Natalie. The concerned look on his face caused her chest to squeeze. "Are you okay?"

"Yes."

He closed the distance between them and brought her into a hug. His strong arms wrapped around her and she buried her face in his chest.

"She doesn't know what she's doing," she said quietly.

"No, but she's dangerous. To you. To herself. To others. She could end up killing someone or getting killed. She'll get the help she needs this way and she'll be off the streets."

He said the words low and under his breath. His calm voice washed over her.

The sheriff secured Susan inside the back of the cruiser.

"Do you have the keys?" he asked.

Natalie put them in his hand. He unlocked the Jeep and retrieved the knife.

"This belongs to her," he said to the sheriff, holding the knife flat on his palm.

The sheriff retrieved an evidence bag and asked Jack to carefully slide it inside, which he did.

"She's the last person I should be trying to defend, but she's suffering," Natalie said.

Jack slid his arm around her waist, and she leaned into him. He leaned down long enough to feather a kiss on her lips before whispering, "That's one of the many reasons why I love you."

She almost believed that she couldn't have heard him right. Did he say love?

It was probably the stress of the evening that had her hearing what she wanted to hear rather than what truly came out of his mouth.

Jack had almost lost Natalie. He took a minute to let those words sink in as he listened to Natalie give her statement. His was next and it matched Natalie's, so giving it didn't take long.

The thought of never seeing her again struck him in a deep, dark place. Natalie was the light and he realized that his last name wasn't going to change but she didn't have to take it. She could take whatever last name she wanted to be as long as she was willing to give him another chance. And he meant a chance at forever.

This wasn't the right time or place to ask. So, he settled on, "I'd like to take you inside."

She nodded and he helped her into the Jeep. Her feet were cut up and her hand needed a field dressing at the very least. Even walking a short distance was a bad idea without proper care.

"On second thought." He reclaimed the driver's seat and turned toward her before starting the engine. "The ER might be a better first stop."

"These are superficial." She looked at him with the most intensity he'd ever seen in those cobalt blues. "I want to go home. Except I don't know what that means anymore. Because your house is the closest I've felt to belonging somewhere since losing my only family."

"Okay. We're going home." He figured home was a good place to start.

The drive to his garage was short. He cut off the engine, parked, and then closed the garage door. He exited the Jeep and was by Natalie's side in seconds.

"It might be easier if I carry you." The thought he'd be carrying the woman he loved over the threshold was enough to make him smile. He hoped to do that with intention in the near future. Right now, it was purely for practical purposes. Her feet were cut up. He was strong enough to lift her, so no worries there.

"Okay." She leaned toward him and he easily scooped her up and out of the seat. "I got the door."

"We'll get you in the bathroom where you can start cleaning up those wounds. I'll need to board up the broken window. Any idea which room?"

"No. Sorry." She closed one door and opened another leading into the house.

"Don't worry about it. I'll figure it out." He easily moved into the master bedroom and then the adjacent bath, setting her down on the counter next to the sink. He located a first aid kit that he kept underneath the sink along with a couple of fresh hand towels. "These should get you started. I'll be back in a few minutes."

True enough, he had a hammer and some small leftover plywood pieces that would do for tonight. With Susan incarcerated, he wasn't worried about another break-in. Boarding the windows was meant to keep bugs out and provide some small measure of security.

Natalie's words kept looping through his thoughts as he secured the back door. This place felt like home to her. *He* felt like home to her. A seed of hope took root deep in his chest that they could build on those sentiments.

There was at least one barrier, and it was an important one. His last name. He was a McGannon through and through. He didn't want to be anyone else. Jack couldn't be happier with his family and heritage. It presented a problem for Natalie, which was a problem for him. Even if he offered to take her last name, the media would be all over it.

Since family was everything to a McGannon, Jack included, it was a relationship problem. So, he hammered the nails into the board, securing it to the door and keeping out mosquitoes, which were a thing basically year-round in Texas.

And when he was finished, he put the hammer inside the junk drawer before heading down the hall again with a glass of water in hand.

Natalie sat at the sink, tending to her wounds. The water in the bowl was clear, so there was no sign of blood. He took that as a good sign her wounds were superficial and that she hadn't been downplaying her injuries.

"I'm pretty good with a bandage. Mind if I help?"

She sucked in a breath and he realized he'd startled her.

"Sorry." He set down the glass of water in his hand, and then put his flat palms out toward her. "Didn't mean to catch you off guard."

"It's pretty much my life. Is it sad to say I'm kind of used to it?" She picked up a hand towel and dried her hands then her feet. "And I'd love some help because I'm terrible with bandages."

Jack moved into action. Her admission struck him square in the chest. Living in constant fear was no life. He stood by and watched as she smoothed ointment on her skin, thinking there had to be some way to help.

Providing security twenty-four-seven wasn't the best option. A good shooter could hit her from a distance. Hiding on the ranch would be too limiting. She needed to have the freedom to move around the state and the country.

He made a mental note to do a little digging into the Fontenot crime family. It was possible he could negotiate a bargain for her freedom. Everyone had a price and Jack had more money than any one person could ever hope to need. Putting it to good use sounded like a great idea to him.

As he mulled over possibilities, he was also struck by her inner strength. It was time she knew how he felt.

"You're amazing, Natalie. You never cease to surprise me with your kindness and beauty. And I don't just mean what you look like. Yes, you're beautiful but it runs so much deeper than outer looks."

Her cheeks flushed and damned if it didn't make her even more attractive. The fact she didn't see herself as gorgeous only served to improve her looks. There wasn't anything self-centered about her.

"I think you're pretty great yourself," she said on a smile that sent a lightning bolt straight to his heart. With one look, she could bring him to his knees.

He'd take it.

No need to push for more than she was ready to give. No need to rush on his part. In that moment, he was content to just *be* with her.

Picking up the bandage, he leaned in for a kiss that sent more of that electricity firing through him. He cracked a smile as soon as they pulled apart.

"What?" Her cheeks turned a darker shade of red.

"Nothing. Happy." Those were the only two words he could form while standing in the haze that was Natalie.

17

"Thanks for letting me stay over." Natalie practically beamed at Jack. She could feel the energy radiating from her smile. It felt so good to smile and mean it.

His answer came in the form of a grunt.

"What?" Her attempt at being nice didn't pan out the way she'd figured it would.

"I hope we're beyond politeness at this point." He cracked a smile.

She laughed. It wasn't even all that funny. It was more a release of pent-up stress. She could exhale and that felt so good right now. "This has been one for the record books."

"It sure has." He'd finished wrapping her feet and had moved onto her hand. "This one won't require as big a job."

He pulled a good-sized band-aid out of the first aid kit, ripped open the package and placed it over the cut. His rough hands could be so gentle. She missed the feel of them on her body and the things they could do to bring her to the tip of ecstasy.

Not really a good train of thought while Jack was so close, she could reach out and touch him so easily.

"Much better." She pulled her hand back a little too fast and the move caused a reaction from Jack. "We should get some sleep."

He mumbled something that sounded a lot like he was agreeing with her. That low rumble of a voice washed over her and through her.

"Can you walk okay?"

"I'm good. The balls of my feet took the brunt. I can use some help down, though." She eased to the floor, holding on for dear life. It wasn't as bad as she feared it might be. Pressure on the right foot went okay, so she risked the left. All good there too.

Jack held his arm out and she grabbed on. He was like a metal bar, stable and strong. She managed the short walk to the bed, thankful she'd already freshened up and brushed her teeth. He joined her after doing the same.

Lights out, he slid under the covers. She moved beside him, curling her leg around his while settling in the crook of his arm. Taking in a long, slow breath, she breathed in his spicy and masculine scent.

Closing her eyes, she could have sworn she heard the words, *I love you,* whispered in the darkness.

Tonight, she slept hard. When she woke up, the sun was peeking through the blinds and she was in the exact same spot as when she fell asleep.

"You awake?" Jack's sleepy voice sent awareness skittering across her skin.

"How long have you been awake?" she asked.

"About an hour, give or take."

"You didn't get up?" She knew he was used to rising early

on the ranch. Four a.m. was his magic number. It had to be six-thirty at the earliest.

"Nah. You looked content and I didn't want to wake you."

Well, now he really caused her heart to squeeze. "That's really thoughtful. Thank you. I slept like a log. Hope I didn't snore too loudly."

"It wasn't bad."

Oh, great. So, she did actually snore? She'd just thrown that out there hoping he'd tell her she was crazy.

She shifted her weight to free him. He took a few seconds to push up to standing. He checked his phone on the nightstand.

"Bernie had a good night. Looks like Derek will be able to operate today." Jack held his cell toward her so she could see the pic of Bernie resting.

"Think we can stop by first. I'd like to see him before he goes under. Give him a kiss and a little encouragement." She didn't know how much dogs could really understand in a situation like this. She knew for a fact Bernie understood a few words. She hoped he could feel her energy and read her emotions. She wanted to provide any comfort she could.

"I bet he'd like that. I'll put on coffee and then we can head out. Maybe grab breakfast on the way over. There's a really great breakfast taco truck—"

"You had me at taco." She laughed, feeling so much lighter this morning. Yes, part of the reason was the fact that Susan was behind bars and would no longer be a threat to Natalie, Jack, or herself. Then, there was the promise they would make certain she got the help she needed.

But the rest of it was being with Jack again. There was a sense of lightness and fun whenever he was in the room. He was adventure and a feeling of the world being right again. Forget about sex appeal because he had that in spades too. The *thing* that had made this relationship special was the feeling of trust she had with him. She trusted him with her life and her heart. That was such a rare feeling for Natalie, and probably a casualty of being on her own for so long with no one to depend on.

Natalie forced herself to get up and move into the bathroom. Her feet were surprisingly better after a good night of sleep, proving the cuts weren't very deep. She freshened up, redressed her wounds, and then changed into fresh clothes that had been laid out for her from the dryer. On her way out of the bedroom, she almost tripped over her backpack. Her life savings were inside. The backpack also reminded her of why she'd been on the run in the first place. Roch Fontenot had sworn revenge for his father. Jack's last name was still news.

Being so in love with someone she could never have was worse than awful. It was soul crushing. Her chest squeezed like she'd been zipped into a vest that was four sizes too small. Breathing hurt.

She would never knowingly put Jack in danger. He would want to protect her. So, the best course of action was to gather up as much strength as she could muster tonight, and then walk away.

The best way—the *only* way—to make certain he didn't follow her over the proverbial bridge was to set it on fire after she crossed over.

～

JACK HUMMED. No, seriously. He caught himself humming as he made two cups of coffee. *Humming.*

Having Natalie here was making him ridiculously happy. So much so, he was making music. His step was lighter. The world had a sense of rightness about it again. After the breakup, he'd missed everything about her. For survival's sake, he'd learned to shut down those feelings. Bury them deep.

He'd been successful.

He heard her footsteps padding into the kitchen. Coffee in hand, he turned to face her with what was probably a ridiculous smile on his face. One look at her was all he needed to know something was wrong.

Her smile didn't reach her eyes. Speaking of which, her gaze stayed trained on the rim of the cup like she couldn't bring herself to meet his. All his internal warning bells sounded.

"Everything okay?" He handed over the coffee.

"Fine." She took the cup and forced a small smile.

He went from humming to bumming in T minus four seconds. He'd seen the same look in her eyes the day before she ended their relationship the first time around. This wasn't the direction he was hoping for.

While she was getting ready, he made a phone call that he thought might change her mind. Now, he wasn't so sure.

"Can we go straight to see Bernie?" she asked.

After a quick cup of coffee, they were on the road and headed toward Derek's office. Silence sat thickly between them inside the Jeep. Once they entered Bernie's room, the mood changed.

"Hey, boy." Natalie made a beeline for Bernie and gave him a hug. If that move didn't hit Jack in the solar plexus, he didn't know what would. Seeing the two of them together, one word came to mind...*family.*

Could he bury those feelings twice? There might not be a choice.

On the flip side, she'd been through an ordeal. Maybe

she needed a little space to process the events of the last few days, especially last night. Either way, he planned to be there for her as long as she needed him.

Rather than go out to eat, he ordered breakfast tacos for delivery. Twenty minutes into their visit, his cell buzzed. The delivery guy was in the lobby. Jack excused himself and met the driver.

He thanked him and offered a generous tip. Cash.

"Hey, thanks a lot, man." The driver studied Jack. "Do I know you?"

"Nah. Probably not."

"Are you sure?" The guy checked the name on the order and then rocked his head. "Oh, right. McGannon. I'm sure I've met people in your family before."

The McGannon name would always be with Jack. Don't get him wrong, he was proud of his last name. It just came with a price.

"There's a lot of us," he joked.

The driver smiled.

"Must be nice," he said.

"It is."

The driver took off and Jack walked into the exam room, tacos in hand.

Natalie looked up. Her eyes were red-rimmed. Had she been crying? Well, now he really was on full alert.

"Want to talk about it?" he asked, pulling a chair beside her and offering food.

She shook her head before taking the taco.

"Okay. I'm content to sit here with you. I like being with you, Natalie. And if you want to talk, I'm here for that too."

This time, her smile was authentic. She nodded but didn't speak. He could guess what was on her mind. Instead of going down that road, he ate a quiet breakfast with her.

He threw the trash away as his cell buzzed again. This time, indicating a phone call.

"This is important," he said by way of excuse as he left the room and walked into the parking lot. He answered on the last ring before the call would roll into voicemail.

"I have news for you." Felix Sanz was a topnotch private investigator. "I think you're going to like it."

Jack listened intently, saying a few uh-huhs into the phone. He finished by saying, "And you're one hundred percent certain this information is true?"

"Yes, sir."

"You're a genius, Felix. I appreciate this."

"You might not say that when you get my bill." Felix laughed.

"Don't I get a friend of family discount?" Jack teased.

"I'm charging you double." More of that laughter filled the line.

"I'll happily pay this bill," Jack said.

"Glad I could deliver for you, man."

Jack ended the call after thanking Felix for the information—information that he hoped would change a certain person's mind. There was only one way to find out. He took in a sharp breath and walked inside the building, across the lobby, and into the exam room.

"I just got off the phone with a private investigator my family uses." Felix's name wasn't important. "He did some digging."

A look of panic crossed Natalie's features. "What did he find?"

"Roch Fontenot is dead."

She gasped, which caused Bernie to lift his head despite his comfortable position of being scratched behind the ears.

"That's right. The Fontenots had a rival. Louis Guidry.

His family took over for the Fontenots, but not before taking out his son. They called it tying up loose ends. Anyway, your testimony put Thibaut Fontenot behind bars and that's what gave them the opening."

Her mouth nearly hit the floor. "It's over? No one's coming for me?"

"If anything, they would thank you."

"I'm not sure any of that's a compliment, but I like the part about not living in fear anymore." Those cobalt blues stared up at him. "That's why I was upset before, Jack. I don't want to leave. I'm in love with you."

"I don't think I've ever stopped loving you, Natalie." He dropped down on one knee. "I've never loved anyone the way I love you. You're it for me, Natalie. You have my heart lock, stock, and barrel. I don't need to look any further for the person I know in my heart I'm meant to spend the rest of my life with. Would you do me the incredible honor of marrying me?"

She stared at him with a poker face that gave away nothing. His pulse raced and his heart hammered his ribs.

And then she glanced at Bernie.

"Don't you mean marrying us? Because if Bernie isn't part of the family..." Her face broke into a wide smile and his heart sang. "I'm so in love with you, Jack McGannon. I can't wait to be your wife."

"You've made Bernie one happy dog." He pulled her up to standing and wrapped his arms around her waist.

"Yeah? He does seem to approve." She motioned toward Bernie, who looked like he was smiling.

"I love you," he said to Natalie. And he couldn't wait to start working on forever.

18

EPILOGUE

Dalton McGannon stepped inside the back porch of the big house, and toed off his boots. He lined them up perfectly with the pair next to them before turning toward the door leading to the kitchen. Anticipation mounted and his mind bounced all over the place wondering about the announcements his father was about to make.

Out of the corner of his eye, he saw his brother, Jack, and his future bride, Natalie, walking toward the house. Bernie, their rescue dog, sat like a king as he was being pulled in a wagon that had tires twice the normal size. *Better shock absorbers*, Dalton thought. Too bad there were no such inventions for navigating life's trickier situations, like the reason their dad had cheated on their mother.

Dalton stopped long enough to hold open the patio door for the trio, and patted Bernie on the head as he passed by. He was a sweet boy.

"How's the recovery going?" Bernie had recently undergone surgery for hip dysplasia.

"Good. He's strong and that helps a great deal. Aren't

you, Bernie?" Jack smiled and Dalton would swear the dog returned the gesture.

"Any idea what all this is about?" Dalton nodded toward the kitchen door. Although, two questions were on everyone's mind. Why did their dad cheat on their mother? And, was Uncle Donny an active participant in their dad's accident or an innocent bystander as he claimed?

Both questions burned and had the power to change Dalton's opinions about two prominent figures in his life.

"None. I know as much as you do, which isn't much," Jack admitted, putting his hands in the air, palms out. "It's anyone's guess what's going to be said in there."

"Have you spoken to Reed and the others?" Reed was their oldest cousin.

"Not me, but Levi might have."

"It's weird not being able to discuss the elephant in the room." Dalton's family might not be the overly talkative type but they'd always been tightknit. There weren't many secrets between them.

"Agreed."

Dalton figured that was as much as anyone could say until they learned the truth about what happened in the equipment room that day. He directed his attention at Natalie, and smiled. After growing up in a family of all boys, it was strange having so many new female faces in the group. "Good to see you again."

"You too, Dalton."

"And welcome to the family, by the way. I promise we're not always this..."

"Interesting?" She smiled and Jack's face lit up as he looked at her. The two seemed to have found the real deal with each other and were goofy in love. Good for them. Jack and all of Dalton's other brothers had, in fact, found the loves of their lives. The new joke was that there had to be something in the water.

Dalton wouldn't touch that faucet with a ten-foot pole.

Jack caught Dalton's gaze.

"How do really feel about hearing the reason Dad cheated on Mom?" Jack's question was legitimate as far as Dalton was concerned. Their dad remained completely devoted to their mother during their marriage to hear Miss Penny tell it. If he didn't know her to the core, he'd be tempted to call her out. She was one of the kindest, most honest people he'd ever meet. To hear Miss Penny tell it, their father worshiped their mother. He spoke of her often, especially around the holidays, and always with the utmost respect in his voice. So, what happened? Another nagging question returned. Was it any of their business what happened between a husband and a wife?

"I've gone back and forth on that one. Part of me agrees with Levi. If Mom forgave Dad, then who are we to weigh in on their marriage? The strange thing is that I've seen the hollow look in his eyes and can tell he misses her to this day." He shrugged. "But, then, maybe I'm just seeing what I want to. You know?"

"I tossed and turned all night thinking about it too," Jack admitted. "Since I can't seem to stop thinking about it and wondering why he would do such a thing, I guess I'd rather walk in there and find out. Maybe get some kind of closure."

Dalton nodded. His thoughts had been running along similar lines. The temptation to find out and put the subject to bed once and for all was too good to pass up. Then, there was their brother Kurt. The man had made it abundantly clear that he didn't want to be part of the McGannon family from day one. Except that he had an adorable daughter who would have had zero family if anything happened to Kurt.

His reasoning for answering Uncle Donny's claim ran deeper than surface level. Kurt wasn't asking for anything for himself. All he wanted was his daughter to have relatives to count on should anything happen to him.

It was noble in Dalton's book and the family had welcomed both him and Paisley with open arms. That was the thing about being a McGannon. The name came with responsibilities others could only imagine but it also came with the love and support of the entire clan.

And that was a large part of the reason everyone wanted answers about Uncle Donny's possible involvement in their dad's fall. A cavern was dividing the close-knit family, pitting cousins against cousins. No one was talking about it yet. No one seemed ready to tackle the elephant in the room...in *every* room now that Uncle Donny had been arrested.

Not addressing it was causing the wound to fester. So, it felt like a no-win situation until they got answers—answers he hoped his father would be providing in a short while.

"Guess we better head inside and find out what this is all about," Dalton finally said.

Jack issued a sharp sigh. What they were about to hear might divide the family forever if Uncle Donny was guilty. No one wanted that to happen. No one wanted Uncle Donny to be capable of attempted murder. No one wanted the aftermath that would come as certainly as heat in a Texas summer—aftermath that could break the family apart forever.

Jack cleared his throat and put on a smile. "Whatever it is, it'll work out."

"Always does." Dalton wanted those words to be true more than anything. He looked to Natalie as he moved to the back door of the house. "Ma'am." He made a show of welcoming her in.

"Thank you, sir." She beamed back at him before walking inside.

"Be careful drinking the water around here. You might just end up finding your soulmate," Jack teased as he walked past.

Yeah. Right. And pigs fly.

Dalton stepped inside the house and the hum of conversation hit him first thing. He'd lost count of how many vehicles were parked in the lot next to the big house and it wouldn't do any good to try to count heads inside, considering there were so many new additions to the family the room was full.

Dad was there, sitting at the head of the table, nursing a cup of coffee as he often did before dinner. It was good to see him up and around even if he was taking it slow with his recovery. Of course, if it was up to him, he'd be working the land already. Thankfully, he'd listened to reason and his doctors.

Miss Penny walked over to him and whispered something into his ear. He smiled up at her when she was finished. Clive McGannon was the strongest man Dalton knew. His father had seemed herculean growing up. Strong as an ox didn't begin to cover it. He was also known for being fair, and his employees were lifelong. Most became like part of the family. So, seeing him in his current condition was a gut punch. It made Dalton think about how short life could be and how fast it could turn. Something that felt a lot like longing filled his chest. But longing for what? He had everything he could possibly want in this very room, and he didn't need or want the complications of a relationship. Dating around suited him just fine. Besides, he couldn't go there with anyone, not after losing a piece of his heart.

"If everyone could settle down for a second, I'm afraid I have disappointing news," his father began.

The room quieted faster than a starving dog eating his food, and suddenly the mood changed from lighthearted banter to tension so thick it was palpable.

"Everything okay, Dad?" Levi, the oldest save for the new guy, asked.

"Yes. I'm all right. I just wanted to be upfront with everyone. Paisley's come down with a fever and Kurt won't be able to make dinner." Concerned voices filled the space. "It's probably nothing. Just a cold with a slight cough. He reassured me the doctor said she would be fine in a few days."

A collective sigh filled the room and it warmed Dalton's heart to see how easily everyone had accepted the little girl.

"As you can imagine, I'd like to hold off on making any announcements until the whole family is together. So, eat. Stay. Talk. But there'll be no news from me today. I apologize. Know that I fully understand how much you want and deserve answers." In true Clive McGannon fashion, he said, "But food's getting cold and Miss Penny whipped up some of her best dishes. Go ahead and fill your plates."

It took a second for anyone to move. Levi took the lead, starting the line around the kitchen island as others followed suit.

Disappointment filled Dalton and it was more than just the cancellation of his father's announcement. There was something deeper, more primal. Something that felt a lot like unfulfilled need, which made no sense and wasn't something he wanted to explore on a good day, let alone now.

And to make matters worse, he couldn't pinpoint where it was coming from. So, he sighed before walking over and taking a plate. He struck up a conversation with his cousin

Reed, hoping the man's father wasn't about to be locked up for the rest of his life.

Dalton couldn't help but think there were sentences far worse than life behind bars.

To keep reading Dalton and Brielle's story, click here.

ALSO BY BARB HAN

For more of Barb's books, visit www.BarbHan.com.

ABOUT THE AUTHOR

Barb Han is a USA TODAY and Publisher's Weekly Bestselling Author. Reviewers have called her books "heartfelt" and "exciting."

Barb lives in Texas—her true north—with her adventurous family, a poodle mix and a spunky rescue who is often referred to as a hot mess. She is the proud owner of too many books (if there is such a thing). When not writing, she can be found exploring Manhattan, on a mountain either hiking or skiing depending on the season, or swimming in her own backyard.

Sign up for Barb's newsletter at www.BarbHan.com.

CPSIA information can be obtained
at www.ICGtesting.com
Printed in the USA
LVHW111406090621
689797LV00012B/274